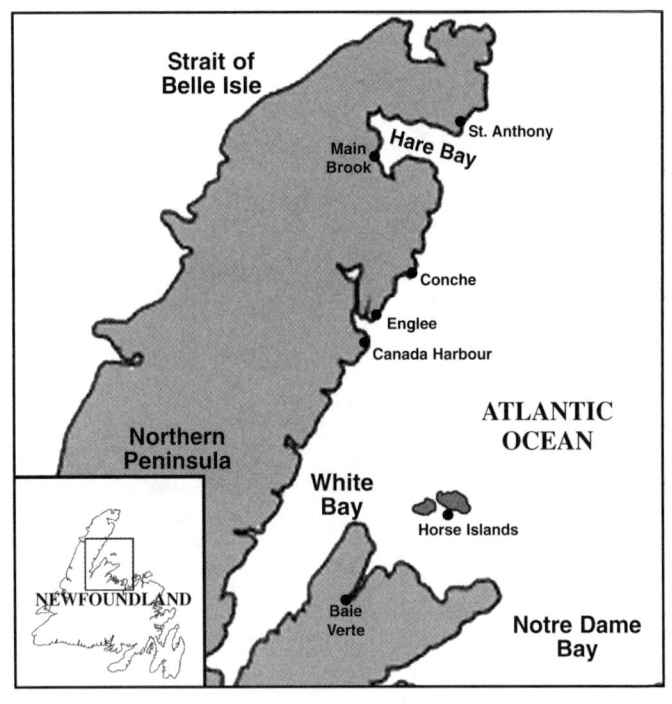

The Day of Varick Frissell

Earl B. Pilgrim

National Library of Canada Cataloguing in Publication

Pilgrim, Earl B. (Earl Baxter), 1939-
    The Day of Varick Frissell / Earl Pilgrim.

Includes index

ISBN 0-9734669-0-1

1. Frissell, Varick--Fiction. 2. Viking (Sealing ship)
3. Shipwrecks--Newfoundland and Labrador--
Fiction. I. Grenfell Foundation. II. Title.

PS8581.I338D39 2004   C813'.54   C2004-900134-5

Front Cover photo is Varick Frissell and his dog Cabot
Back Cover SS Viking

Published by Grenfell Foundation
and Bough Wiffen

PRINTED IN CANADA BY PRINT ATLANTIC

Distributed by
~ DRC Publishers ~

3 Parliament Street
St. John's, Newfoundland and Labrador A1A 2Y6

Telephone: (709) 726-0960
E-mail: staceypj@avint.net

PRAISE FOR EARL PILGRIM'S
"The Day of Varick Frissell"

"A great read! Earl has done it again. His craftiness at weaving fact and fiction together brings one of Newfoundland's earliest disasters to the forefront. Many people of my generation have never heard of the Viking disaster, let alone the fact that Paramount Pictures actually filmed the seal hunt in the 30's.
A must for anyone who has kept up with Earl's adventures. A real page turner to the very end!"

Ernest Simms
Mayor of St Anthony

"Earl Pilgrim has demonstrated once again that he is truly a master of that genre of literature known as historical ficton -a novel based on established historical facts. The Day of Varick Frissell is the story of the Viking Disaster of March 15, 1931, related in detail by the ghost of Frissell himself over seventy years after he died in the disaster. The suspense and intrigue in this story is both innovative and magical and grips the reader from beginning to end. As well, this novel established once and for all that the Viking Disaster was caused by carelessness and plain stupidity with the end result that twenty-seven men lost their lives."

John Parsons
Author and editor of Probably Without Equal:
Frank Mercer and the Newfoundland Rangers (2003)

"Using a mixture of fictionalization and dramatic first hand accounts, **The Story of Varick Frissell** tells how a young American filmmaker galvanized the attention of respected international explorers as well as a major Hollywood studio and made an epic film on location in the frozen North Atlantic with Newfoundland sealers. Earl Pilgrim's reconstruction of the last days of the SS Viking's final journey in 1931 offers sincere testimony to those whose lives were lost in one of many tragic marine disasters off Newfoundland shores."

Victoria King
Documentary filmmaker, White Thunder

Preface

The loss of the Viking is a well known Newfoundland tragedy, one of so many which in so many ways have defined this island and the people who dared to live here. Now we have the story brought back to life by Earl Pilgrim. And though it's not always easy going -- was anything in Newfoundland ever easy -- we are fortunate to have this retelling of the tale.

It goes without saying that Newfoundland is an elusive kind of place -- a northern land perched precisely and perversely and precariously on the edge of the dominant warm and cold ocean forces which are the life blood of the land, the yin and yang, or if you prefer, the blessing and the curse. Similarly elusive are the Newfoundlanders, a relentless people who ever mindful of their somewhat dubious providence persist and persevere to make a life of it all, a life which both defies easy depiction and draws much admiration.

The northern Newfoundland ice fields are even more elusive. They shift and heave, break up and reform, flow freely then jam tight. They stun you visually and entice the uninitiated. Only a very few highly selected forms of life survive there, and even then only for very short periods of time; the ice fields are not hospitable to humans and yield their treasures reluctantly. Yet this is where Newfoundlanders would go each year to hunt the seals.

Young Varick Frissell was not the first to succumb to the charms of Newfoundland, the North and the ice. Like thousands of others he chanced upon Wilfred Grenfell and set out on a rite of passage which became the definitive adventure of his life. But Frissell was different. He was not content just to have the memory and to talk about it; he wanted the world to see and hear it just like he had. He had the vision and the passion, he knew the story, he had the means . New photographic and audio techniques would make it all possible. This was his time. This was his day. Others shared his dream and joined his venture. His first efforts had great promise, but he needed more. So with primitive film making tools in hand he was off again to the ice in an old iron-clad wooden wall, shipmates with a crew of Newfoundland sealers and too much cordite.

This is a classic tale and in Earl Pilgrim we have the quintessential Newfoundland storyteller telling it. Larger than life himself, Earl has an eye for the place, an ear for the people, and the voice to bring them alive and together again.

So here we have it -- a great raconteur and a great Newfoundland story.

Enjoy The Day of Varick Frissell.

~ **Peter Roberts**

ACKNOWLEGEMENTS

Without the help of Mr. Gary Newell and the Grenfell Foundation, this book would have not been written.

Special thanks to Harry Steele for reading the manuscript and giving advice.

I would like to say thanks to Lt.-Gov. Edward Roberts for reading the manuscript.

A special thanks to the Newfoundland and Labrador archirves and their staff for helping with research.

Thanks are expressed to Frank Mercer of Bay Roberts for helping with the story.

To the late and great Paddy O'Neill, who helped with research but passed away before the book came into print, "Thanks Paddy."

Thank you to Varick Bacon for permission to use Frissell family photographs.

I would like to thank Victoria King for reviewing the contents of the manuscript and supplying material, and
a special thank you to Jean and Peter Stacey for editing this book.

A special thank you to the following people: Bill Maynard, Bob Ropson, Caesar and Barbara Pilgrim, Baine and Nancy Pilgrim, Tom Maynard, Tom Canning, Stanley Compton, Jonnie Dempsey, Leander Hancock, Perry Compton, Wilfred Curtis, Roger Short, Junior Canning, Ivan and Mona Manuel, Kent and Elizabeth Brophy, Mark and Michelle Brophy, Norman and Marsha Pilgrim.

And to my wife, Beatrice, I would like to say a very special "thank you" because without her help this story would not have been completed.

A special thank you to Dr. Peter Roberts for writing the foreword. A former executive director of Grenfell Regional Health Services, he is currently a member of the Grenfell Foundation Board.

Chapter One

The little speedboat gently touched the sandy beach on Green Island as the wildlife officer tilted the outboard motor up.

"The boat should not hurt here, Nicholena, " he said.

The young girl standing in the front of the boat looked back and smiled. She hadn't understood some of the words he'd said earlier due to his Newfoundland accent.

"Oh my," she said, "what a beautiful beach. The sand here is almost white."

The officer had stepped ashore here many times but due to his workload he had never noticed the colour of the sand.

"Yes," he said. "It does look kind of white."

Not concerned enough about the beach to comment further, he jumped out into the water and took the painter and threw it ashore.

"My dear, I will have to carry you ashore to keep your feet dry" he said.

"That will be great, but give me a minute to get my pack-sack on and get my shovel."

"Sure," he said.

She knew that this broad shouldered ex-Canadian Army Commando would have no problem carrying her one hundred and twenty pounds for about twenty feet (She had been told by Gary Newell, head of the Sir Wilfred Grenfell Foundation, that he had also been the light heavyweight boxing champion of Canada). Very confidently, she climbed upon his back and was carried ashore.

Green Island is a small flat rolling land mass located at the western end of Grey Islands, Newfoundland. The island got its name because in summer it's completely green with grass, flowers and all kinds of berries and shrubs.

During the summer it is the home of many different kinds of nesting sea birds, including approximately eighty per cent of all nesting eider ducks around the island of Newfoundland.

It was, in fact, the eider ducks that brought the young university student, Nicholena Leonardo, here for a planned three weeks. Nicholena was from New York City and for the past four years she had been studying at Yale University. Her studies were mostly about the effects of oil dumping on sea birds, especially in relation to eider ducks off the coast of northern Newfoundland and Labrador.

While researching this project she came in contact with the name of Sir Wilfred Grenfell and his Mission in northern Newfoundland and Labrador.

She then contacted the president of the Grenfell Foundation, Gary Newell, who knew of an eider duck project in progress.

The people involved gladly agreed to have her for the summer. She soon packed up and flew to St. Anthony, Newfoundland. Now here she was on this beautiful day standing on the sandy beach of Green Island.

She heard the sound of many different kinds of birds as she stood ready to work on the eider duck project that was already under way, and sponsored by Ducks Unlimited (DU). Canada.

Nicholena was a beautiful girl with long blond hair. She came from a Swedish and Italian family who were in the restaurant business in downtown New York City.

Nicholena had no interest in the restaurant business she was destined to inherit. At an early age, she was fascinated by the wilds of nature and soon convinced her parents that she wanted to become a wildlife biologist,

The road to this spot on Green Island had involved much study. She was glad now to begin the practical part, "in the wilds of nature" as she referred to it.

John Christian, the wildlife officer, better known as, "the game warden," knew what had to be done: the nesting boxes had to be repaired and some had to be moved. The heavy seas that had rolled in last fall had washed the rocks off some of the boxes, causing them to be moved from their proper places. Now, every box had to be looked into, the nests and eggs tallied, and as many birds inspected as possible.

After the warden had explained everything to Nicholena they walked around the island to the areas where the nesting boxes were situated. In all, there were approximately thirty five hundred nesting boxes on the small island.

Nicholena knew full well she had her work cut out for her, but she was smiling and happy to get the chance to work in such a beautiful place as this and said so.

The officer took her to the outside part of the island, close to the water, and suggested she should begin here and work her way around toward the boat and she agreed.

"Some of those boxes are too close to the water. Every year the sea does damage to them. Maybe we should move them farther back," he said, then thought a minute and added, " But maybe for the duck's sake we should leave them here for another year at least.

"Okay, my dear," he continued, " you will be all right alone on this island. There is nothing here that will hurt you."

Looking at his watch he said, " It's noon now I am going to go in over the center of the island and have a look at the caribou herd. We have to find out more about the young calves. I should be back around six this evening if it's okay."

Glancing at her he added, " Are you used to working alone, my dear?"

She looked at him and smiled, "No problem," she said "I will be a busy girl here today. I have the cell phone with me, if I want you, I'll call."

"Good," he said "I think you have my number, 709-457-7339."

"Yes, thanks, I've got it," she said.

He shook hands with her and said, "Have a good day. I will be watching the weather."

With that, he turned and headed for the boat.

Chapter Two

The sky was a pale blue on this warm sunny day. Nicholena walked upon the small hill that overlooked the roughly 200 acres of nesting ground surrounded by the mighty North Atlantic and called Green Island.

With all of her fury in some of the worst storms ever unleashed, Mother Nature has not been able to sweep the island away. Damage her, yes, but not beyond repair.

And, with all the many billions of tons of pressure from the mighty ice fields reaching all the way from Greenland and driven into her by the strongest current on earth, "the Arctic Current," yet this crunching, thundering force has not been able to move her one inch.

As Nicholena looked around with admiration, she silently whispered "What a place, yes, what a place."

She watched the wildlife officer as he headed in toward Grey Islands Harbour, the sound of the outboard motor fading gradually away.

They say most every place on earth is filled with mysteries. Things happen every day that never get recorded. And it is a known fact that people look around in places where they know things of importance have happened, and say, "If this land could only talk." So it is with Green Island.

Nicholena Leonardo was a brave girl and known not to shy away from any challenge big or small.

On this day, she was dressed in a pair of working shorts and t-shirt, with a small packsack on her back. In it, she carried a portable CD player with headphones and a couple of recordings by Don Williams. She also carried her movie camera, a small pair of binoculars, her cell phone, and her lunch for the day. She had her notebook and pencil in her t-shirt pocket.

As she walked along the grassy slopes carrying a shovel she wondered aloud saying it was vain of her to even think about what this chunk of rock and soil had seen, that it was something only the gods would know.

With shovel in hand, the young New Yorker strode quickly to the outside part of the island where a line of duck boxes snugly hugged the ground. As she got closer she was excited by the sight of so many old eider hens flying out of the boxes and landing safely on the water.

"This is what I came here to see," she said, "I think I should take a picture of this," then decided not to because she wanted to get directly at the work.

She noticed that this particular line of boxes was laid out in a kind of a valley approximately twenty feet from the area where the sea hove in when there was a storm on.

"Is it any wonder that all the rocks that keep those boxes in place are gone? I bet they were washed away by the sea during a storm last fall," she said. After putting down the shovel and taking off her packsack, the first thing she did was look under the boxes for signs of nesting eiders. What she saw was breathtaking, every box had a nest or two and the egg count ran from two to seven.

She didn't disturb anything and only kept the boxes up long enough to do the necessary paper work, then put them back again in their proper place.

"My oh my," she said, "I have never seen anything like this before, even this is worth coming here. What I have seen in those boxes is worth it all."

She decided to put rocks on top of the boxes to keep them in place, "I am going to have to bring rocks up from the beach," she whispered, but then she saw the beach rocks and knew they were too heavy for her to lift. The rocks near the boxes, however, were much smaller and although they were partly covered over by sod she decided it was better to dig them out than try and bring large ones up from the beach. First, though, she would have some lunch.

Sitting down on one of the nesting boxes, she opened her packsack, took out her CD player and inserted a recording. "Lord I hope this day is good," rang out the voice of country singer Don Williams and the whole area seemed to almost come alive.

She noticed the white flowers all around and knew what they were immediately because she had studied botany. They were cloudberries, known locally as bakeapples.

Her heart was full of joy as she ate her sandwich, then energetically started digging out rocks to put upon the boxes.

She peeled back the sod and began lifting the small rocks out of the hole she was making.

"Lord have you forgotten me?" sang Williams as she worked.

Then she saw something.

"That doesn't look like a rock," she said out loud as she hooked at it with the top of her shovel. "Something white?" she said as she bent down and looked closer, "It's not a rock, that's for sure, must be a piece of wood."

She put down her shovel and started rooting around it with her fingers. It was round and smooth. Then she realized what it was.

"It's a bone of some kind."

She looked again then started scraping it with her fingers.

"A bone from something that's for sure," she said out loud.

She removed some more material from along the bone, "It's a large bone," she whispered.

She took off the CD headphone she was wearing and placed it on the nesting box near her, forgetting to turn the music off.

Her attention was now caught up in the large bone she was uncovering.

"I don't think it's a seal's bone," she said.

She dug gently again until all the bone was uncovered; then very carefully removed it from its resting place. Examining it more closely, she realized what she had found.

It was the leg bone from some human being. There was no mistaking that. She had seen this kind of a bone in the laboratory when she was studying anthropology.

"My" she said. "I wonder if there are any more bones here near this."

She put the femur bone on the nesting box and started digging again.

It didn't take her long to find the lower end of a pelvic bone.

"My," she said again. "There's probably a complete human skeleton here."

By now she didn't know what to do.

"Maybe I shouldn't dig at this anymore. I could be disturbing some poor soul from their rest."

For a moment she didn't know what to do. She heard music playing on the CD player.

"I wonder if the warden is still at the cabin or if he's around the harbour?" she asked herself.

She put down the shovel and walked up the hill which overlooked the entire area. Not seeing or hearing anyone, she came back down to where she had been working and sat down.

"Yes," she said, "I think I will uncover the whole skeleton if there is one here."

Sweating by now she wiped her forehead, then, kneeling down, she began the task of peeling back the sod that covered whoever it was that was lying in this unmarked grave.

Nicholena had made up her mind that she was going to see the complete skeleton of whoever was there. She forgot about the eider ducks and the nesting boxes. She didn't hear the voice of Williams or notice the flowers that seemed to be silently watching her. Her mind was transfixed on one job and that was to uncover the human frame that lay in front of her.

"Oh God" she prayed silently, "forgive me for this in advance if I am about to wake up the dead."

She was surprised when she realized that she felt a little ill at ease. "IMAGINE, FOOLING AROUND WITH HUMAN BONES." This thought echoed around and around inside her head as though it would never stop. She felt fear rising in the pit of her stomach.

When the sod was peeled back she began to remove the rocks that covered the skeleton. She first uncovered the legs and feet and was shocked when she discovered that the bones in both lower legs were broken and even crushed.

"This person must have been in some kind of an accident or something," she said when she saw the sight.

"I would say that this is the body of some poor sailor who was shipwrecked or got swept overboard out in the Atlantic many years ago. Probably he got tossed upon the shore here by a giant wave. But," she concluded, "the body came to this spot intact because every bone is here."

She looked at the bones of the feet and was convinced that they must surely belong to a man because of their size.

When she had finished uncovering the lower legs, she began to take the rocks, mud and sand away from the pelvic area. This was much easier to do because the ground was softer. It took Nicholena two hours to remove all the material from the skeleton. She could hardly believe she had the nerve to do such a thing, especially seeing she was alone.

"Imagine uncovering someone who has been in their grave for many years," she said aloud.

She took the large femur bone that she had earlier removed from the skeleton and put it back in the same place.

"Will I ever get forgiveness for this?" she cried loudly as she sat back on one of the nesting boxes and stared at what she had uncovered.

"I think I will take a few pictures of this," she said as she reached for her camera.

It was then that Nicholena heard something. She thought she heard someone call,

"I guess the wildlife officer must be coming," she whispered to herself.

She stood up and was about to walk up to the small hill when she heard the sound again.

Immediately she knew that it was not the officer, it appeared the words were coming from among the bones.

"What am I seeing and hearing?" she asked herself in a frightened way as she stared at the bones. "Am I about to hear the dead talk?"

She decided to run away from the scene, but couldn't. She could only stare.

"Dear God" she cried in agony. "What am I about to hear, or see?"

Nicholena sat down on the nesting box and stared at the skeleton. It was then that she heard a voice, and it was coming from the bones that lay in front of her.

The voice said, "Don't be afraid of me, young lady. I am not going to hurt you. I just want to talk to you and ask you to do me one favour if it's possible."

The voice sounded kind, and very gentle.

She said afterwards while telling her story, "It was a voice that took away any fear I had."

She said she must have nodded yes, because the voice said, "I am now going to stand upon my own two feet as a man, the same as I was before that terrible explosion on the Viking."

There was a pause as she stared in wonder at the bones.

"Am I going out of my mind?" she asked herself loudly. "Or am I dreaming?"

The voice spoke again. "You are neither, do not fear. All will be well for you."

There was a pause.

She stood up and noticed that her legs were shaking.

The voice spoke again. "I want you to look westward for a moment. When you turn around you will see me as I was."

He repeated, "Don't be afraid of me, you have nothing to be afraid of."

She immediately turned her back to the skeleton and looked westward. She heard a rattling noise. Then all was quiet. She knew she would have to turn around, and slowly did.

Nicholena Leonardo said she would never forget what she saw on that day. As she turned around she was face to face with a tall, well-built man. He was very handsome. He stood facing her, smiling. She found herself walking toward him and saying, " How do you do sir?"

He held out his hand and gave her a warm handshake. "I'm Varick Frissell," he said.

She looked up at his face then said, "I am Nicholena Leonardo, how do you do?"

"Just fine," he said slowly.

She recognized his New York accent, and for a moment wondered who he was.

For a moment, she forgot about the skeleton she had dug up, and was carried away by the handsome man she was looking at.

Then. her mind raced through the halls of her memory as the name Varick Frissell flashed before her.

"Varick Frissell," she stammered. "You mean Varick Frissell of the White Thunder movie?"

He looked at her with dreamy eyes and knew that this girl had heard of him. He then replied. "Yes, I am Varick Frissell of the movie White Thunder."

She had seen and read all the literature about him while studying at Yale. She had read the plaque placed on the university wall in memory of him. And, she had seen his movie.

He had graduated from Yale in the 1920s and gone on to become a movie producer for Paramount Pictures.

Yes, she knew all about him, in fact everybody in her class and at the university knew about him.

But it was beyond her wildest dreams that she would meet face to face with him. She felt goose bumps rise all over her body.

He again reassured her that all would be well. She was not to worry.

Varick beckoned Nicholena to come and sit near him on the nesting boxes.

She looked at him. Then, without hesitation, she came and sat down near him.

He appeared as though he was about to sit at a table on the balcony of the greatest resort in the world. He was very relaxed and happy looking.

She sat three inches from him, close enough to hear him breath, and almost close enough to hear his heartbeat. Close enough, in fact, she could feel the heat from his body.

"Do you mind if I ask you some questions?" he asked.

"No sir," she replied shyly.

"Nicholena, you don't have to call me sir. Just call me Varick. That's what all my friends and the Newfoundlanders call me. It will make me happy."

"Okay, Varick, you can ask me anything you like. If I know the answers I will gladly tell you."

He smiled and thanked her.

Varick looked into her eyes, then said, "I can tell by the look of the clothes you're wearing that you are living in a different era then when I was living. Tell me what year this is, my dear. I mean what is the present date?"

She looked at him and knew that he was anxious to hear her reply, " This is June 2002."

He almost stopped breathing as he hung his head and looked into his huge hands. "2002," he slowly replied, "I have been here in this place for more than seventy-one years."

He pointed to the grave where she had found him. Nicholena looked at him, he looked so real. He was not the kind of ghost or spirit she had read about many times.

She could not see through him. He was there in person. He looked so real, yet he was a man from out of the past.

"Another question I want to ask is, do you know who is now the president of the United States of America?"

She told him that she was an American from New York and knew all about America.

"George W. Bush is now the President, a Texan. He used to be the Governor of Texas and an oilman. He was also a Yale graduate, the same as you were."

"Well," he said, "after all."

Then he lifted his hand high in the air. "I never thought it." He turned to her and said, "I guess you could call me a Newfoundlander now because I have been here for so long."

She did not question his statement.

He asked her another question, "Tell me please, is there a war of any kind going on now that America is involved in?"

She wanted to tell him about the war on terror and about 9/11 but she couldn't, with the flowers around them so beautiful and the sunbeams warm and bright. They were also sitting in one of the quietest places in the world. She decided to keep quiet about it all.

But, in answering him, she said, "There will always be wars and strife, Varick, until the end of time."

"Yes I guess you're right, my dear," he paused, then said, "I'm sorry that I asked you that question, I might have known the human race will never learn."

There was a silence.

She watched him carefully as he stood on his feet. In reading about the life of Varick Frissell it is always noted that he was a very handsome man so it's little wonder that Nicholena's heart leaped as she studied him with admiration.

Varick motioned towards the equipment that she had taken out of her packsack.

"What is that you got there, my dear?" he asked gently.

She reached down and picked up the small video camera that she had taken out of her packsack and lodged on the nesting box.

"That's a video camera or you may call it a movie camera."

He looked at her with wide-eyed wonder, "A movie camera. What do you mean?"

It must have given him quite a shock when he saw it. Imagine that to him it was yesterday when he had been using a camera on the Viking that was so large and heavy that it practically took two men to lift it around. And now here was a camera that you could almost hold in the palm of your hand.

He picked it up and looked at it then put it down again.

"I will give you a demonstration," she picked it up and put on the "on" switch.

"Can I focus the camera on you, Varick?"

"No, my dear, you can't. You see, people will never believe you when you tell them what you are now experiencing, let alone seeing it."

"Okay," she said as she aimed the camera on one of the flowers that grew about twenty feet away. She focused carefully as he watched her. She asked him to talk to her as she filmed the flower.

"I will show you what I just filmed," she said.

She pulled out the screen latch and showed him the beautiful bakeapple blossom she had just filmed.

It was then that he heard himself talking. He listened and watched dumfounded. She could tell that he was almost in shock, especially when he saw the beautiful color on the small screen.

He took the camera from her again and looked it over, "I don't believe it," he quickly said as he handed the camera back to her. Then he noticed the CD player, near the packsack.

"May I ask you what that is," he asked, pointing toward the gadget.

"That is a CD player. It's a machine that is used to play music."

He again looked with wonderment.

"If you don't mind, I will put the ear phones on you, and you can listen to the music," she said and he agreed.

She put the headphones on herself first, and tuned in Don Williams singing. "Lay down beside me and don't ever wonder away."

She stepped closer to him and reached up with the headphones. He was a tall man 6 ft 8 inches. When she reached up she had to place her body close to his. Varick Frissell could not resist this beautiful girl. He put his arms around her and kissed her and she did not resist him.

As Williams started to sing this beautiful song, she saw a big tear fall from his eye and onto her arm.

He reached up and took the headphones off and handed them back to her, then wiped the tearstain from his face and gave a sigh. "There's no time for this my dear," he said. "Come closer, Nicholena, I want to point something out to you."

He was looking toward the ocean in the direction of the Horse Islands.

She moved close to him as she stood up. She wanted to put her arms around him but hesitated, not knowing what to expect. He shaded his eyes and stared in the far off distance.

"Do you see those two islands out there?" he asked, pointing.

She looked closer then replied, "Yes, I can see them."

"Well," he said, "they are the Horse Islands."

Nicholena looked.

Then he said, " Not far from the Horse Island is where it all happened. I am going to tell you about it, in fact I am going to tell you a story that no one else has ever heard. It's about that frightful night on the Viking seventy-one years ago." He caught her by the hand and said, "Come along with me onboard the Viking."

Chapter Three

Varick Frissell was born in 1903 and grew up in New York City, a member of one of New York's most influential families. His father, Dr. Lewis Frissell, was a distinguished businessman.

Varick and his younger brother, Monty, were very much alike. They were adventurous, hard working, tremendous outdoorsmen and inseparable.

There was no doubt that Varick was quite a ladies' man. He got involved with girls at an early age and charmed everyone he came in contact with. His friends said this was mainly because of his tremendous voice.

After high school he joined up with a band and toured many parts of the States as the lead singer. He sang country, the blues and sometimes opera.

He was so good at singing opera that he was persuaded to try out at the Metropolitan in New York. However after his try-out session nothing further was heard of this afterwards. For Varick, the Opera House could not compete with his love for the wilds of Newfoundland and Labrador.

Varick was also quite good as a guitar player. It was said that this is what made him so popular with Newfoundlanders.

He would play and sing and entertain hundreds of sealers while on sealing ships at the ice fields, usually singing the songs of Jimmy Rogers and Tex Ritter.

Varick possessed great stamina. Men who worked with him often told of his great ability to cut logs using a cross cut saw while he was working as a volunteer with the International Grenfell Association in Newfoundland and Labrador. It was said that he once spent twelve hours manning a pump on the deck of a sealing vessel, during a winter storm while heading for the ice fields.

He was recognized in the city of St. John's, Newfoundland, and around the small towns on the Great Northern Peninsula. He was known as well up and down the coast of Labrador where he spent a lot of his time. Whenever he was seen walking the roads people wanted to shake his hand. It's said everyone in Newfoundland who knew him loved him.

Varick's first contact with Newfoundland came one night, during the summer of 1923, when he was invited to attend a lecture by the famous Sir Wilfred T. Grenfell, the renowned medical doctor who spent most, if not all, of his life giving medical aid to people in northern Newfoundland and Labrador. Grenfell started the International Grenfell Association, an organization recognized worldwide.

Dr.Grenfell gave a slide presentation on his work in northern Newfoundland and Labrador and Varick was so impressed he stayed behind and met him personally. This first meeting with Grenfell impressed him so much that it changed his whole life, and from that time on he became a devoted supporter of the doctor and his medical mission.

Varick was invited to come to the little village of St. Anthony, Newfoundland, home of the Grenfell Mission, the following spring. Doctor Grenfell gave the young New Yorker a job overseeing installation of a water system for the Grenfell medical complex there. This was a giant project that kept Varick at St. Anthony for two years.

During the winter, he used dog teams to haul timber and

firewood out of the forest for the Mission, and to build two dams for the water system.

Varick was a member of a well known New York family and destined to take over the family business. Like every other CEO of all large corporations, a well-known name sometimes gives a lot of creditability and prestige when it comes to acquiring growth in the world of big business. So it was that many of the up and coming sons and daughters of these families went out and took on different things to make a name for themselves or to become well known. Some, for example went into politics and made their mark, others went into the sports world and became Olympians.

Their subsequent reputations opened a lot of doors in the business world. These fields, however, did not interest Varick Frissell. He was looking at something else.

Varick became interested in the movie picture fad, which was one of the most popular movements of the 1920s. He soon got involved with home movies and became an expert in camera work. His trips to Newfoundland and Labrador led to Varick becoming obsessed with filming.

First he started filming the people around the coast and in the small settlements where they fished and hauled cod-traps. He filmed the lumbering town of Roddickton where Dr. Grenfell had a large steam driven sawmill.

One day, Dr. Grenfell came to Varick and asked him if he would like to go north to North West River, Labrador, to install a water and sewer system at his medical mission there. Well, of course, the young adventurer accepted without hesitation.

By now, Varick saw the great potential in filmmaking and hired a cameraman who accompanied him to Newfoundland and Labrador.

During this time he took a lot of film of the area, especially the ice fields, and the giant icebergs that rolled and tumbled along the coast every spring and summer. He realized that this was something that should be shown to the world.

When Varick Frissell was at North West River, he heard

people, mostly Indians and trappers. talking about the giant waterfalls located many miles inland on the great Grand River (later the Churchill River).

The excitement and determination to film this waterfall became more apparent every day, and Varick knew it had to be done and he would be the one to do it.

In the winter of 1925, Varick got the finances from his father, assembled equipment necessary to put together a film crew, and went off to Labrador to film the great falls.

At Yale that winter he met up with a young man by the name of Jim Hillard whom he hired to go with him on the filming trip.

The trip up the Churchill River was a grueling and frightening experience for Varick, Hillard, and the two guides from Labrador, John and Bob Michelin of North West River.

It was, however, a tremendously successful piece of film work that they did. In fact, it was so successful that it gave Varick membership in the National Geographic Society and the Explorers Club of America.

Varick told a reporter afterwards that while they were filming the Grand Falls he was lucky he didn't get swept away into eternity, indicating he must have had a close call.

This was no doubt due to his daring and adventures attitude, especially around the steep cliffs and canyons of the mighty Grand River.

When Varick arrived back in the States with the film footage of the Grand Falls it was soon shown in theatres everywhere.

Varick became such a supporter of Dr. Grenfell that he started touring Europe with him, lecturing and showing the film of the Grand Falls. Twice, he accompanied Grenfell to England and used the film as a drawing card to fill the halls.

Varick always had an urge to make home movies. He dreamed as well of making a full-length movie, and of course this film that he made of the Grand Falls only strengthened his dream.

Many prominent people in the film industry, in particular the great filmmaker Robert Flaherty, saw the film that he made of the falls and were impressed.

Flaherty recognized a great potential in what he saw and knew that this young up and coming Varick Frissell was a genius. He immediately contacted him.

After this, Hollywood came knocking on his door.

Chapter Four

Varick was obsessed with the great winter seal hunt that took place every year off the coast of Newfoundland. He went out once as a hired hand, seeing what it was like to be a sealer working on the rolling ice floes with a spiked gaff in one hand and a hauling rope in the other, working from early dawn till sunset.

He knew what it was like to be in a bunk wrapped in a single blanket in the middle tier of a forecastle with a hundred more bloody, greasy and unwashed men.

He knew what it was like to have to go out in the middle of the night and look for someone who had not returned before dark, using lanterns and torch lights, listening to the horn blaring out the signal for the searchers to return in the event the lost soul is found.

Varick proved that he was as tough as anyone on board, and for this the Newfoundlanders loved him. He was known as Doctor Grenfell's man. He even helped give medical attention to many while out on the ice floes working at the seals.

Varick was a very strong man. It was said that he was the strongest man on board the sealing ship. Although it was never proven in any kind of a contest it was obvious because of the large number of seal pelts that he would take in tow at one time and drag to the side of the ship, or to a pan of ice where they were stacked and flagged to be picked up by their mother ship. They said he was a giant. He also walked slightly bent over.

After having first hand experience on sealing vessels and working and seeing the hardship that those hardy Newfoundlanders toiled under, Varick was determined to make a full-length movie of the seal hunt.

He knew the drama in watching men jumping from ice floe to ice floe and sometimes finding themselves down in great valley waves like canyons, then being lifted high into the air by the next wave and still standing upright on moving pans of ice. All this, while doing their job as if they were in a cornfield, somewhere on the prairies.

He was certain the American public would be thrilled by watching this, even without dialogue or any kind of a script or story. Just to watch those daring Newfoundlanders perform their work under such conditions would be worth the money. This alone would be enough to entertain any audience and hold them spellbound for hours.

Chapter Five

Because he had such a love for Dr. Grenfell and his medical mission, Varick decided to go back to St. Anthony for a year. During this time he started to install a water and sewer system for the hospital. This was not a small task due to the lack of proper construction equipment. The work was done mainly with manual labor.

All the blasting was done by Varick himself. He was quite familiar with using explosives. The year before he had helped an old sealer blast a sealing ship through an ice field without even cracking the paint on her bow.

During the winter he was working in St. Anthony, Varick received a letter from Paramount Pictures stating that the company was not interested in making a motion picture based on the seal hunt alone.

"There would have to be a story of some kind," they said.

"This is what the American public wants, and that is what they would pay their money to see."

Varick was quite taken aback by this but he knew they had the last say in making the film. He sat down and talked matters over with Dr. Grenfell.

Grenfell, with his experience in giving advice, advised Varick that this would be a greater challenge for him.

"The task of writing a script and then directing the making of the motion picture is a new venture for anyone," said the wise old doctor.

Varick then sat down in his little room in St. Anthony. It took him a few days to come up with a plan for a story.

"What do you think the American public would like?" he asked Grenfell.

"Well, Varick," he said, "what would you like to see mixed in with an adventure story? Because this is what they are saying in Hollywood: Give us an adventure story not a documentary, something similar to the westerns, only you're going to have it happen on the ocean among the Arctic ice. Instead of cattle and trains, you're going to use seals and ships."

"So, in other words, Doctor, you're saying that I need to write a script about a love story that is say…a young sealer out on the ice fields having to leave his girl friend back home or something similar?" said Varick excitedly.

"Now you are on the right track, young man," the doctor laughed. "I can see it now. Sealer goes wild over his lover while out to the ice fields and tries to kill a fellow sealer who is also in love with her, or something similar."

Varick shook the doctor's hand.

"I still think that there is enough drama and excitement in just the seal hunt alone to make it a great selling motion picture," he said. "However, they are the ones that will put up the money, and I guess they probably know what they want."

As he left he said, "A love story, that's it. I will write a love story about two young fellows in love with the same girl, say up in Harbor Deep, who go fighting over her out on the ice field during their trip to the seal hunt. That should make a great story."

It took about two months for Varick to write the script for the movie he named "White Thunder."

In early June, he went back to New York and sent his script to Hollywood and Paramount Pictures.

It didn't take long for them to reply that they liked the script and were prepared to go ahead with the project. Varick was excited and was soon on his way to Hollywood by train. He was hired by Paramount and put under the guidance of Robert Flaherty.

He was sent into New Mexico to help direct a film about the Pueblo Indians. This gave him a lot of badly needed experience. In a letter to his mother he said it was quite an experience to watch Robert directing.

Varick must have been a fast learner because he was given the go ahead to direct the White Thunder picture that was scheduled to start in the winter.

The preparation for such an undertaking as the making of the motion picture White Thunder was quite a task. Actors had to be selected, rehearsals had to be undertaken, equipment and material had to be assembled.

The leading role of Luke, the hero of the movie, was played by Charles Starrett, who was featured in some 130 B Westerns. From 1937 to 1952, he was listed among the top ten money-making Western film stars.

The leading role of Mary Joe was played by Louise Huntington who appeared in this and other feature films,

Harry Sargent was also an actor and helped Varick direct the film.

Arctic explorer Capt. Bob Bartlett played a sealing captain named Cap'n Barker.

There were also 15 other people in the film crew.

Arrangements with the owners of the sealing vessel Viking, owned by Bowring Brothers Limited of St. John's - one of the major shareholders in the movie company Varick formed - had to be contracted and confirmed.

Varick was a very busy man. He moved to St. John's where he opened an office in the King George V Seamen's Institute on Water Street, the oldest street in North America. Paramount Pictures gave the Institute a generous donation. Dr. Grenfell gave Varick the complete second floor of the west wing of the building for his use. This included three single bedrooms, one double bedroom and a large reading room. He also had two more bedrooms, which he quickly converted into offices.

The offices that Varick occupied on the second floor gave him a complete view of the Narrows and the Harbour of St. John's. Varick said many times that he was a happy man whenever he set his feet in the capital city of the colony.

St. John's was booming in 1930. The fish merchants were at their peak, and the sealing fleet was bringing in bumper loads of seal pelts like never before.

Varick Frissell and the White Thunder motion picture was the talk of the town. Excitement was everywhere on the streets of St. John's.

Chapter Six

It didn't take long for the long and hungry month of March to roll around. The movie people had everything in place. The sealers had all come to St. John's. They were briefed at meetings as to what they would have to do and how they would have to act in order for the movie crew to get their job done.

The most important thing the sealers had to do was to carry on as if there were no cameras on board, being cautious when the actors were doing their scenes on the ice.

Varick's main camera work would be to get shots of men working on the ice while huge swells were rolling, and icebergs tumbling and foundering. Of course, blasting the ship through the ice fields using explosives would be another scene.

Members of Varick's movie crew included fellow Americans, Harry Sargent and A.E. Penrod.

In 1925, while Sargent was a young student at Yale, he attended a lecture given by Dr. Grenfell who immediately recruited him to come to St. Anthony and work as a volunteer at the medical mission for the summer.

Sargent says that while he was hitch hiking from St. John's to St. Anthony on fishing schooners he met up with Varick

Frissell and Jim Hilliard at Twillingate, Newfoundland.

The two were going to Labrador to film the Grand Falls. Due to poor connections, Harry got marooned with them for a week. He said later that it was the best thing that ever happened to him. Harry got to know Varick and the two of them became very close friends.

Harry noted that Varick was a man with a very good sense of humor and said he had a real sense of imagination and vision.

"Varick saw beauty in the simpler things of life," said Harry, who followed his career from the first day he met him because of his admirable qualities.

Harry Sargent was an able man, there was no doubt about that. He came from a family of strong able-bodied women and men. It was thought that this was the reason the two became such good friends from the first time they met.

They were both tall and handsome. They attracted women wherever they went. For instance, while the three young Americans were marooned at Twillingate and Lewisporte for a week they were wined and dined by the ladies of the towns.

Varick, of course, carried his guitar and played and sang cowboy songs. There were times when they literally put off shows for the people. Everyone knew that Harry was a volunteer for the Grenfell Mission, some even thought he was a doctor. They all knew as well that Varick and Jim were on their way to Labrador to make a movie picture.

Chapter Seven

The winter of 1930 was not a cold one in St. John's. But there was a lot of snow and this gave ideal conditions for Varick to make his movie about sealing and sealers.

The cast for the movie and camera people and equipment operators were all staying in hotels around the city. All went well as Varick proceeded on schedule. Most of the filming was done just outside St. John's around the little fishing village of Quidi Vidi.

The American film crew and the New York actors were well looked after. They were very excited especially when they were reminded that this film was the first one to use Hollywood style sound film outside the sound studios.

In mid-February all the "on land filming" was done. Varick notified Paramount Pictures that this was completed, and everything was ready to start preparations for filming out on the ice fields.

But, before the Viking went to the sealing grounds she traveled to St. Anthony on a filming trip. This gave Varick the opportunity to see Sarah, the girl he had been dating there for the past two years.

Varick was anxious to start out to the sealing ground. He just couldn't wait to get out there. With his experience as a sealer on two previous occasions he found himself no different then the rest of the Newfoundlanders. The seal hunt was in his blood. He was obsessed by what went on out there. And now, on this trip, he would be filming the very thing that kept him fired up for a full year, the seal hunt.

At the end of February, Robert Flaherty came to St. John's. He was very pleased with the job of directing that Varick had done on the film to date.

He was also amazed at what Varick had done as far as being the first company to use sound-synchronized films on location.

After giving the work an A1 rating, he wished everyone the best, had a party, and then went back to New York and Hollywood with a good report.

Chapter Eight

The Viking was a gallant wooden ship of 620 tons, built in Norway in 1881 and purchased and brought to Newfoundland strictly for the seal fishery by Bowring Brothers Limited in 1904.

From 1904 to 1926, she was under the command of William Bartlett senior. He was one of the famous Newfoundland sealing captains, and with him as skipper the Viking brought in well over 222,000 seals.

The Viking had most of her houses constructed in the rear section. The captain, officers and any special guests on board had living quarters in that same area, mostly under deck.

There was also a dining room and saloon in that area, and right in the very back of the ship was the cargo area.

In the front of the ship. there was what the crew called a forward forecastle. This was where the ordinary, everyday sealers slept and ate.

The bunks were built in tiers, sometimes as many as four tiers high with approximately two feet between bunks. A large table ran up the center of the forecastle and a stove fired by coal stood propped up on four crooked legs. This rickety stove kept the water boiled to make tea, and provided much needed heat in the forecastle.

There were two sets of large hatches, which they called the forward hatch and the rear hatch. When the ship was in motion the hatches were covered over with the usual covers made of wood, and a large canvas tarpaulin over each secured with wedges.

The Viking had a hull of solid oak 18 inches thick. This was covered with half-inch iron sheeting screwed onto the oak. This sheeting came almost to the bulwarks. The ship was built to withstand the grueling, grinding Arctic ice.

The Viking was powered by a huge steam turbine, had two boilers and was pushed with one propeller.

When Varick Frissell went to Delaware and put together "The Newfoundland and Labrador Film Company" he knew that it would not be an easy road. However he had no trouble raising the finances and securing a contract with Paramount Pictures. A lot of his investors were Newfoundland businessmen, including Bowrings, the chief shareholders.

With financing in place, he realized his greatest problem would be in securing the cast for the film.

He met Dr. Grenfell at New York. where they went over the complete plan. Varick was worried because he didn't think that Captain Sid Jones was the right kind of actor for the job

He had tried him out earlier on the set during the winter and had found that his voice wasn't suitable for the kind of sound equipment they were using.

"I wonder who I can get to play the part of the captain, you know, someone who has a reputation at the seal hunt and has a voice that is not to ...say, squeaky?"

Dr. Grenfell listened with interest, then replied, "I know of such a person if he will agree to do the part."

Varick waited for Dr. Grenfell to finish.

"Captain Bob Bartlett," said Grenfell. "You should ask him."

Varick knew at once that Captain Bob would be the man. There was no mistaking that.

"I wonder where the captain is now, Doctor?" asked Varick.

"He should be here in New York if my memory serves me correctly," said the doctor.

"Okay, let's you and I look him up," said Varick with excitement.

Captain Bob Bartlett was a renowned man. History has it that without him Admiral Robert Peary would have never reached the North Pole.

Bartlett was born in Brigus, Newfoundland. He commanded his first vessel at the age of seventeen, and the last one on the year he died at the age of seventy-one.

He made numerous trips to the north. He also commanded ships for the United States Navy during the First World War.

Captain Bartlett did Arctic expeditions for almost every Society in North America.

I think I can say without any doubt that Captain Bob Abram Bartlett was Newfoundland's greatest mariner of all time.

Dr. Grenfell and Varick met Captain Bartlett in the dining hall of the hotel where the captain was staying. Grenfell knew him well. They had met many times at St. Anthony and once at Battle Harbor, Labrador, where Peary was coming south in the Roosevelt after his first attempt to the North Pole.

Bartlett was one of the first to come within just a few miles of the North Pole, someone who, after being shipwrecked, drifted from the Belford Sea to the shores of Siberia and lived to tell the tale.

Varick and Dr. Grenfell found themselves in front of this renowned king of the ice fields, someone who had to eat his dogs in order to survive on the ice caps of the far north.

Varick was now ready to put a proposition in front of Bartlett. He said he wanted Bartlett to be an actor in a history making motion picture, White Thunder, that would be seen around the world for generations to come.

It was a generous contract that Varick Frissell offered Captain Bob Bartlett and immediately he accepted.

"I never thought that I would be offered a job such as this," he said with a hearty laugh, adding, "there is one question that

I want to ask you."

"Sure," said Varick.

"Who will be commanding the Viking? I mean who will be in charge of the everyday working of the vessel?"

"Captain Sid Jones," said Varick quickly.

Varick was a little nervous of what Bartlett would say.

"Great. I am glad of that because we are good friends," said Bartlett then asked, "When will I be leaving for St. John's?"

"Tomorrow morning, I will get a ticket for you to Halifax. The next day we will head straight to St. John's."

Bartlett was glad to hear this, because, for one thing, he was going back home.

"Sounds great to me. The only thing is I am going to have to cancel some of my appointments that I had coming up. There should be no problem with that."

"When we get on the boat to Halifax we will go over the script that you are supposed to do," said Varick. "Then I will outline the whole project to you."

Captain Bob gave the okay and said, "I will be ready for you to pick me up tomorrow at the proper time."

The three men shook hands and Grenfell and Varick left.

Chapter Nine

Captain Sid Jones laughed when he saw captain Bob Bartlett walk into the office at the King George V Institute in St. Johns.

"Well, what have we got here?' he said with a laugh as he held out his hand.

"How are you, Sid?" asked Bob Bartlett.

"Just fine," said Jones. "To see you here now makes me feel on top of the world, that is, if you are going to play the part of that sealing captain in the movie picture."

Varick laughed as the two men joked around.

"I never thought that I would ever see you a movie actor, Bob," Jones said with a grin.

"No more then I did," said Bob.

"If you start going around with Varick Frissell you could be involved with almost anything," said Jones, laughing.

March 1930 began with a hectic schedule, the weather turned mild and not much snow.

The plans were made for the Viking, when she would leave port and in what direction she would head.

All the supplies and stores were loaded onboard.

Equipment for killing seals included gaffs, hauling ropes,

knives, sharpening steels and sharpening stones.

Every man was issued a small kettle and a thin water bottle, and a belt to string some of the items on.

Some of the men carried homemade creepers that they would strap onto their boot bottoms to prevent them from slipping around on the rough ice.

On board the Viking were two hundred and thirty eight men, including the captain and officers.

They were from almost every part of the colony. Their ages ranged from fifteen to sixty. They all met on the fifth of March in Bowring's warehouse. They were told when they signed on that they would be part of a crew that would be making a motion picture called White Thunder.

It was clearly pointed out to them that only the actors would be involved. Their aim was to get as many seals as possible. The more seals they got, the better the movie would be.

When Varick, accompanied by his large Newfoundland dog, Cabot, and Captain Bob Bartlett walked into the warehouse where everyone had gathered, all the men cheered loudly.

Not all of the men had seen Captain Bartlett before, but they had heard talk of him and his great work. There was no doubt about it; his name was a household word around Newfoundland.

Varick was in a different category. A lot of people had heard of him but only as a movie producer and a Grenfell man.

They had heard about his famous dog Cabot, and about him singing and playing the guitar. But he was also known as a strong and able sealer, who had been proven out on the ice.

Varick knew how to handle people and what he would have to do to get everyone fired up. He would introduce Captain Bob Bartlett first. Just the mention of Bartlett's name would make everyone cheer.

He knew how to address this crowd, but he was also smart. He told everyone that the captain would not be going as a sealing captain because he didn't want a rift between the two sealing captains, Bartlett and Jones.

"Captain Bartlett will be going as a movie actor," he said as the men clapped and roared. "And to make it all the better, men, we have a woman onboard who will put makeup on him every day. This will help to make him good looking."

Well, that was enough, the men roared.

It was obvious that this would be a very lively trip for the Viking and her crew.

The Viking, under the command of Captain Sid Jones, left Bowring's wharf on the fifth of March 1930. It was a sunny afternoon. The Viking was all decked out in her full bunting with the Union Jack flying at the top of the mast. But on this morning the Stars and Stripes were flying just under it.

Everyone on the wharves and around the streets knew that the Viking was going to the ice field to make a moving picture, and was carrying a group of movie actors from the United States. And above all else, the famous Captain Bob Bartlett was onboard.

It was said afterwards that Bartlett couldn't understand why the Viking headed in the direction of the Grand Banks of Newfoundland. There was no doubt about it. Sid Jones knew where the seals where and that's were he was going. He was heading for seals, not for the icebergs that were down north.

By the tenth of March, when the season opened and the seals were prime to take, they were "into the fat" as they would say. However this was not what Varick and the film crew were looking for. Sure, there had to be seals, but the drama of the hunt was the most important.

The movie was going to be filled with drama. Lots of heavy ice everywhere, with large icebergs foundering, mountains of rolling sea, and valleys of ice. Men dressed in black, jumping from pan to pan, killing seals. And every step filled with the deadly risk that these men were used to.

The filming of the movie "White Thunder" was all done by the middle of June and Varick was then ready to start editing the film. He knew that he would need the help of his good friend, Robert Flaherty, in helping him get everything ready.

At the end of June he left St. John's with the film and all the equipment and headed to New York.

On arriving there he was advised to take the film and come to Hollywood where the editing would be done.

🏛 Chapter Ten

Robert Flaherty was very excited when Varick arrived at his office in Hollywood. The editing went very smoothly, in fact it went better then Varick had thought it would. But he was not satisfied with the film and said so.

"Well now, Varick my man, what's your greatest problem with it?' asked Flaherty.

Varick replied as he had when he first started to edit the film, "There's not enough drama in the film to capture the American public," he said, adding, " we've spent too much time on the girl and the two young men fighting over her."

Flaherty looked at the film again and again and finally said, "Maybe you're right, Varick. There's no doubt something is missing."

"You're right," said Varick. "People are not going to pay money to see or hear someone giving a speech or throwing a few punches over some gal who is heartbroken in an outport town of Newfoundland. I've said this before and I will say it again, no matter what the Paramount crowd says, what we've got done is not the thing."

Varick appeared to be a bit hot under the collar, "Listen Robert, " he said, "let me tell you what it will take to make this film a smashing success."

Robert Flaherty was no fool; he had been a director in the film business for a long time.

"Okay, Varick," he said. "What do you think I should see in that film that is not there now, that would make me want to write a good review, if I was a reporter with the New York Times?"

Varick stood up and said, "Robert, you were at the meeting that we had a year ago with the people responsible, when I outlined what I wanted to do out there on the ice fields. Let me tell you again what I think you should see in that picture so that you would write a good story if you were a reporter."

Flaherty kept quiet as Varick moved around the office.

"As you will notice in the film, the man who is one of the most popular sea captains this side of Columbus or Nelson, Captain Bob Bartlett, hardly played any part at all in the picture. He didn't do what he was intended to do. For instance, he should have been up on the bridge yelling and screaming to get the Viking moving like those captains always do. We should have been involved with icebergs, I mean the kind that should be rolling over and foundering, and tumbling together. We should have been encountering heavier ice that would block the Viking to a point that we would have to use explosives in order to get her free as I've seen many times when I was out as a crew member."

He looked at Flaherty then said, " We took out two or three tons of dynamite and blasting powder and brought it all back. The very thing that would have created the drama we stayed away from."

Flaherty knew that Varick was right.

"Well then, Varick" he said, "what do you blame it on? Or who do you blame it on?"

Varick sat down again, and said, "We spent too much time on the love story. The general public in the States is not going to pay their money to see two young Newfoundlanders from some rock hole fighting over a girl out there on the ice.

They're looking for something different. They can see all the fighting over girls they want in the Westerns that are filmed around Hollywood. It's drama they are looking for, Robert."

The two men sat in silence for a few minutes then Robert said, "Let's go to a coffee shop, Varick, I want to get this off my mind for a few minutes."

"Okay," said Varick, as the two men left Flaherty's office. Flaherty agreed that the movie picture needed more drama, "What should we do next, Varick?" he asked.

Varick took another sip of coffee then replied, "There is only one thing to do and that is go back to the ice fields again this winter and get more footage of the very thing that we had intended to get last winter."

There was a pause.

"We're not going to be able to release the film that's for sure," said Robert.

"I know," said Varick ,"but I know what I will do."

"What's that?" asked Robert.

Varick thought for a moment then said, "I am going to go back to St. John's with the film and premiere it in the Nickel theatre there. We will see what kind of a reaction we will get from the people of Newfoundland. It should give us some kind of an idea. What do you think?"

"I'm not sure, Varick," Flaherty said with concern.

The two men paused for a moment, then Flaherty said, "It is your money, although your company has a contract with Paramount. If it doesn't work out, you will be the loser."

Varick laughed. He knew what Flaherty meant, but he had no intention of making a motion picture that reviewers would sweep under their feet as trash.

A decision was made right then and there that Varick would go back to Newfoundland and start getting things ready to go out to the ice fields again in the Viking and complete the film about the seal hunt.

"But on this trip," he said, " none of the explosives that we take out with us will be brought back to St. John's unless the job is done and we don't need them."

He said this time he would be taking more advice from Captain Bartlett and less from Captain Sid Jones.

Chapter Eleven

Captain Sid Jones was forty years old when he first took command of a sealing ship in 1927. He was a dependable man as far as getting the job done for the company that he worked for. The first ship that he ever took to the seal hunt was called the Ranger, and that was a successful trip.

It is suspected that due to his success with seals in the winter of 1929, he was given the command of the Viking in 1930, when she set sail to the ice fields with the New York film crew on board from Paramount Pictures.

Bowring Brothers Ltd. was a very successful company in Newfoundland and had been involved in the sealing industry for a long time.

Company ships were very successful in getting to where the young seals were, likely due to the fact they employed some of the best sealing captains of that era.

There is no doubt that the Newfoundland and Labrador Film Company owned by Varick Frissell with shareholders made up of mostly Newfoundland businessmen, some of them owners of the Viking, had chartered the vessel.

Although the contract between Bowing Brothers and the

The Day of Varick Frissell

film company is not available, it is thought by historians that the cost of the charter must have been tied in with the amount of seals taken during the trip.

It is also thought that Captain Jones knew where a large patch of young seals was located near the Grand Banks, and could make a quick and successful trip. This would be money for Bowring Brothers and the crew on board.

Of course the film crew could make all the movies they wanted about men on the ice killing seals as far as Captain Jones was concerned, and this was all that Varick Frissell wanted as far as he knew.

"The Viking got a load of seals. But we, the film company, came in empty handed," was a statement made by Varick to Robert Flaherty in Hollywood.

It was disappointing to Varick that he would have to return to the ice fields in the Viking during the winter of 1931.

When he arrived back in New York from Hollywood he was in a good mood although he knew a lot of additional money would have to be spent on the movie.

He also knew he would have to get in contact with Captain Bob Bartlett, re-hire him as an actor, and go back to Newfoundland and finish the movie.

Varick decided that he would take a weekend trip to Vermont and see Dr. Grenfell after learning that he was in the States on a business trip.

Varick was anxious to have a chat with him, for he knew the doctor would have good advice to give him.

He would take along a copy of the movie of White Thunder that he had edited in Hollywood and show him.

He also took along his gallant Newfoundland dog Cabot. Wherever he went, he took the dog with him. He had got the dog on his way to St. Anthony three years earlier.

At that time, one day while he was in St. John's, he visited the Right Honorable Sir John Middleton, who was the Governor of Newfoundland at the time. The two went on to pay a visit to the Honorable William C. Job, Newfoundland's

Ambassador to the United States. Job was a renowned Newfoundland fish merchant, and on the Board of Directors of the International Grenfell Association (IGA).

During Varick's visit, Job showed him a litter of pups his Newfoundland dog had given birth to and Varick immediately fell in love with them. Fifty-seven- year-old Job gave Varick one of the Newfoundland pups, a male he called Cabot, after John Cabot, the discoverer of Newfoundland and Labrador.

From then on Cabot became the trademark of Varick Frissell. Wherever he was seen, the large black and white Newfoundland dog was with him.

Dr. Grenfell was a lover of dogs and when Varick walked in with Cabot he was immediately taken up with the animal.

"What a noble beast," he said in his distinctive English accent, "You should be proud of yourself, young man, for having that dog with you."

"I am," said Varick proudly. "He is my best friend, in fact he was with me at the ice field when we made the movie last winter. He slept on the foot of my bed the whole time."

Varick and Grenfell soon got into a discussion about the movie and after they had finished their conversation Varick said, "First I am going to show you the complete movie then, after you have seen it, I want you to give me your opinion of what you think of it before I tell you mine."

Grenfell viewed the movie and was quite moved by it. The story fascinated him for the simple reason that he knew quite a lot about it. In fact it was his idea that such a script should be written.

However he knew there was something missing, the same way that Varick knew. The drama was not there. It was not the real seal hunt, as Grenfell knew it. It was not very long after the movie ended that he declared, "You have to go back to the ice fields again, Varick, and finish the picture."

Varick looked the wise old man straight in the eye then asked, "Tell me, what is wrong with it, Doctor?"

Grenfell quickly replied, "The drama is not there. I mean

the icebergs rolling and the ship being tossed around by the ice and all that. You know what I mean."

"I know exactly what you mean," said Varick. "And this is why I have come here to see you. I wanted another solid opinion and you have given it to me."

Varick spent the night with the renowned doctor making plans for the next year, how they would take their cameras way down north and film the Torngat Mountains and the fiords.

Grenfell asked Varick if he had heard from the young nurse, Sarah, he was going out with in St. Anthony.

"Yes Doctor, I hear from her all the time. She writes me every week. I am anxious to see her."

"You have a good girl there, Varick, I think she is in love with you," said Grenfell.

Varick was glad to hear this.

"I am anxious to see her, Doctor, I can't wait to get back to St. Anthony," he said.

Chapter Twelve

Early in the morning, Varick went back to New York. He spent all evening trying to reach Captain Bob Bartlett, only to find out from the hotel owner where he stayed that he had gone north on an expedition for the Smithsonian Institute. He knew that this might create a problem for him because sometimes ships would become caught in the Arctic for years before they got free. He was told, however, that he was not gone to the far north, only as far as Greenland. Bartlett had left word he would be back to New York before Christmas.

Varick decided to send him a wireless asking him to join him again in March on the Viking, when they would go back to the ice fields to finish the movie White Thunder.

But before sending a message, he decided to have a talk with Robert Flaherty. Maybe it wouldn't be important to have Bartlett go with them, perhaps there was enough footage shot of him already. It was drama in the film that was missing, not Captain Bob Bartlett.

It was December when Varick arrived back in St. John's. It was cold and windy as he checked into the King George V Institute. He felt comfortable and at home there.

He ate at a local restaurant just down the street from the

Institute. Although there was a small kitchen in the Institute it was always crowded with people looking for work, and sailors from schooners waiting for a passage home to some outport around the coast. Wherever he went, people knew him and wanted to talk to him about the movie picture and the seal hunt.

It was early December when the Morrissey, Bartlett's 120-ton clipper, came into St. John's harbour. There was no mistaking where she had been. The wooden vessel had just returned from Greenland and looked like she had been dragged through a grinding ice field.

The vessel was powered by a large diesel engine and also fully rigged by sails. At first glance, the Morrissey looked like a fishing schooner. However, upon boarding, the difference was evident. She was built of solid oak for Arctic use, and all fastenings were Swedish iron. Her construction was described as unique.

Varick recognized her the minute he saw her coming through St. John's Narrows. She had all her bunting flying and other schooners and ships in the harbor started blowing their horns the minute they recognized her. They knew that Captain Bob Bartlett was coming into St. John's. He was a very popular man.

The Morrissey had a job getting a place to find a berth, but the captain managed to squeeze her in through a group of fishing schooners taking on winter supplies. It didn't take long before Bartlett was standing in the doorway of Varick's office.

Varick stood up and quickly gave him a hearty handshake, "How are you, Captain Bob?" he asked.

Bartlett replied with a smile, "I'm just fine except for the usual cramps from being cooped up in that small schooner."

Varick laughed, "Sit down, Skipper Bob," he said, then added, "I received your wireless this morning and was expecting you when you came through the Narrows. Wireless, I suppose, is the greatest invention yet."

Bartlett agreed then said, "Too bad my father didn't live to see it. Of course half the stuff we got now the old people wouldn't believe even if they saw it."

Ten minutes later, the two men were having coffee in a small restaurant nearby.

"I got enough information from your wireless last week to know that you were heading back here to St. John's to redo the movie picture, is that right?" asked Bartlett.

"Yes, it was exactly as we had said last spring, you remember?"

Bartlett remembered quite well what he had told Varick and the rest of the actors when they were returning to St. John's after the filming was over.

" Boys, listen to me, you don't have enough footage of the roughness of the seal hunt," he'd said. "Listen to me, the seal hunt is about the harshness, the agony, the tossing to and fro of the ship against men in heavy ice, this is what people will want to see and pay their money for and will even come back to see a second time. They won't pay money to hear me screeching and roaring at men to get them to haul on a cable. Sure the part that I played is important, yes, but the drama and the splendor of the grinding ice is what they want to see."

"Do you remember me saying all that?" he asked Varick now.

"I sure do remember," said Varick, "This is what I want to talk to you about. I am back here again and as I said in my wireless to you, I am going to go out again this winter and get more footage of what you're talking about."

Bartlett stirred his coffee then said with a satisfied look, "Sure is good to be sitting down in a place that's not rolling and not having any water under the table, or having ice grinding in your ears night and day as it passed even in July."

Varick knew what he was talking about. Sometimes the Arctic gets to a man and he vows, when he is caught in the ice or in a tight jam, that he will never set foot on board another vessel again as long as he lives. However, a man like Bartlett knows full well that he will return to the ice fields again even if he has to swim.

The two men talked about the film and about the effect it would have on their lives. They knew that this was their chance to make it right.

"It's now or never, Captain," said Varick, " If we release the movie to the public as it is we will never get the chance to make it into something we will be proud of."

"What do you intend to do, Varick?" asked Bartlett.

Varick thought for a moment then said, "We are going back again in the Viking sometime in March, and this is what I want to talk to you about."

Bartlett looked at him for a minute without speaking, then finally asked, "What do you want me to do?"

Varick knew that this wise old Polar navigator was smart. He had talked to him many times about the movies he saw in New York, and the kind he had heard people talking about and read about during the past five years.

He lived in New York City during the winter and associated with high society. During the summer, he talked and worked with ordinary people on boats from many countries. He had listened to their views about the kind of movies they would like to see, and with all of this knowledge Varick knew that Bartlett was an expert.

The two men sat in silence as the waitress brought them a complete apple pie and placed it on the table.

Then Varick asked him," Would you be available in March to go back to the seal hunt with me and finish making the movie that we started last winter?"

Bartlett took the pie server and lifted a large piece of pie onto Varick's plate then answered, "There is not much that I can say until I see the film. You say you've got it edited?"

"Yes, and I have a copy here with me," said Varick.

"Well, can we have a look at it?" asked the captain.

"Yes we certainly can, I even have a projector," replied a delighted Varick.

"I tell you what, Varick, how about letting all of my crew

onboard the Morrissey see it tonight? I can have them come to the main mess hall tonight at the Institute and you can show it to everyone."

"Yes, that's exactly what we will do," said Varick.

Bartlett was very pleased.

"Better still, Captain Bob, we will make it an evening. I will have someone prepare a lunch for everyone at the same time."

"Good," said Bartlett, then added, "After the movie has been shown, then you and I will have a talk about it."

It was quite a night for the men from the Morrissey. They never thought that they would be treated with such entertainment as seeing their captain on the movie screen.

Between reels, Varick and Bartlett would stop for a few minutes and explain to them what they were going to see next.

When the film was over they all clapped and cheered, there was no doubt they all loved it.

Everyone was treated with a hearty lunch at the end of the film; they thanked Varick for a wonderful night and went back to their vessel, all except Bartlett who continued to sit at the table, drinking coffee with Varick

"What do you think of the film, Skipper?" asked Varick anxiously.

Bartlett was silent for a few moments then said, "Do you remember what I told you when we were out there making the film?"

Varick knew what he was referring to but he wanted to hear the wise old captain make his comments again.

"If you don't, then I am going to tell you again," said Bartlett. He paused, then continued, "Look Varick, people are not going to go to the theaters to see me out there roaring and yelling at a group of rugged men. Some of it you could get away with in order to get the job done and they know it. But blasting through the ice fields and those ice bergs crashing near the ship and the rumble of the ocean against man is what they want to see. It's something different and this is what you've got to add to the movie in order to make it a great one."

Varick agreed, then Bartlett added, "If I was you I would make it perfectly clear to whoever was in charge over there at Bowring's that the Viking would be going where I wanted it to go this year. Not out on the Grand Banks where we went last year. Tell them that you're not making a film of the cod fishery, you're making one about the seal hunt down north."

Bartlett appeared to be angry and Varick shifted on his seat, " What you're saying then, Skipper, is that it's not necessary for you to even go back with us."

"That's right," said Bartlett. "You would be wasting your money to have me do anything else. You can tell by the reaction of the men here tonight that they were excited about the dialogue."

Varick agreed, then asked, "What would you suggest?"

"I know what I would do," said Bartlett, "I would take on a load of dynamite, powder and all the nitroglycerin that I could get my hands on and head north the minute the Viking poked her nose out through the Narrows. Then I would head straight for the Horse Islands area. Or the Grey Islands. Or somewhere around there, that's the place we always called Iceberg Alley. And that is where you would get the job done. There's always lots of seals in that area, it's the real whelping ground."

Varick knew that was right because he had been there a few years earlier when he was out to the ice with Captain Wes Kane.

"There's one more thing that I've got to say before I go back to the Morrissey and that is I would blast the Viking right on through all that heavy ice up there. And if I had to, I would founder every iceberg and I'd knock down every cliff in White Bay. I'd have my cameras mounted on the head of her all the time, night and day. I'd miss nothing. There wouldn't be one ounce of explosives brought back to St. John's. I would use it some way or another, I'd make sure of that."

Varick agreed and Bartlett then told him how to founder ice bergs before he got up and put on his coat.

"All you need is the same crew of cameramen that you had out there last year. Harry Sargent, Noseworthy, Penrod, Fred Best, and yourself of course, that's enough. As I said, I would mount a camera on the bow and stay there night and day if I had to, I'd capture everything."

Varick agreed. That was what he would do.

"I don't suppose I will see you again till next spring. Varick," said Bartlett, who had a lot of respect for the young New Yorker. He always said that Varick Frissell had a lot of spunk and would go places.

Bartlett went on to say, "I received a wireless from Job's agent a week ago, telling me that they would not be needing me to take one of their sealing ships to the ice fields this winter because the markets for seal products is very low. In fact, they said they might not even send any ship out this winter at all." He paused, then said, "I am going to accept an invitation with a group that want me to go to the Antarctic, but that's another story because nothing is finalized yet."

Varick Frissell and Bob Bartlett shook hands and wished each other well, and as quick as Bartlett came he was gone.

Long before daybreak the next morning, the Morrissey slipped out of St. John's harbour. Varick and Captain Bob Bartlett would never meet again.

Chapter Thirteen

Varick sent a telegram to Dr. Grenfell in St. Anthony informing him that he would be arriving there in a couple of days and would like to have a meeting with him regarding the White Thunder movie.

The doctor replied that he was at St. Anthony and would be delighted to have him come and spend Christmas there. With this invitation, Varick and Cabot boarded the S.S. Prospero, a government contracted mail and passenger ship, and headed north to St. Anthony.

St. Anthony in 1930 was a great place to be. From the time Dr. Grenfell made the little town his headquarters there was never a hungry day spent there. Even through the great depression of the 1930's, St. Anthony found itself with full and plenty, and the people shared what they had with others. Varick and Cabot were given a warm welcome when they arrived at the Grenfell town, as it was often called.

Dr. Grenfell was there to meet him along with Sarah, Varick's girlfriend. Sarah was a nursing assistant to Doctor Curtis, then one of the leading surgeons at Grenfell's Hospital. She was a young girl who came from a small town further north. It was very clear that she was in love with Varick. She ran to him and kissed him. In joking about it later, Dr. Grenfell said that it was not a pleasant sight for one of his employees to do such a thing in public.

Twenty-seven-year old Varick told Doctor Grenfell this was the way the Americans did things. "We're not like the English, Doctor," he said.

Dr. Grenfell said, "I know, young man, I happen to be married to an American, thank you," and they both laughed.

Sarah's father was a fishing skipper who was well known around the area and was a supporter of Grenfell's Mission. He had no objection to his daughter seeing the American film director he had met on two occasions.

After Varick had said hello to Sarah, he and Cabot went to Dr. Grenfell's office to talk about the movie. Varick told him he was planning to go back to the ice fields and do more filming. This was no different from what he had told him earlier that fall at Vermont. But he added that Captain Bartlett would not be going, saying he'd talked with Bartlett and the captain had said all the work he was involved with was done.

Grenfell was silent.

Varick went on to say, "We intend to take twice the amount of explosives on board that we had last year. We intend to blast our way through the ice field. This will give the picture more drama."

Dr. Grenfell looked worried, "I am kind of disappointed that Bob Bartlett is not going with you on that trip, Varick," he said.

Seeing he was concerned Varick asked why.

"Well, Varick," said Grenfell, "Captain Bob Bartlett is a very experienced man when it comes to the ice, and especially when it comes to using explosives on the ice."

Grenfell was serious, he knew what he was talking about. He then continued, "You've got to have a good man in control out there when you're using that stuff, Varick. I have seen too many accidents happen where men have got killed trying to blast ships through the ice. This is where Bartlett comes in.

Men are afraid of him. If he tells someone to do something they will do what he tells them."

Varick was quiet. He knew the doctor was serious.

"Robert Peary told me once that the only ship that he was ever on that was under full control was with Bob Bartlett. When you're carrying explosives as you're planning, you have to have discipline. It's the only way."

Varick quickly said, "You don't have to worry about that, Doctor, I've got a lot of experience using that kind of stuff."

Grenfell thought for a moment then said, "It's not you that I will be worrying about, it's the other two hundred that will be onboard who don't give two hoots about anything. And that's the reason I was saying it would be good to have Captain Bartlett with you."

Varick again recognized Grenfell's concern then said,

"I think Captain Bartlett has a prior commitment. He's booked for a winter's exhibition to the Antarctic to carry out scientific research for the American Museum of Natural History and would not be able to go with us even if we wanted him."

It appeared that Grenfell was not satisfied, however there was not much that he could say about it so he let the subject drop. Grenfell then went on to tell Varick the latest news, "We are getting ready for our Christmas program now, Varick, you are just in time. It's going off tomorrow evening. Would you be able to give the audience a talk on the movie White Thunder?"

"Yes, I certainly can. It's too bad I didn't bring the movie and the projector with me, I could have shown the complete movie to the people."

"That's too bad," said Grenfell.

Christmas of 1930 was a very enjoyable one for Varick Frissell at St. Anthony, Newfoundland. He was madly in love with Sarah. The two of them spent most of their time at his quarters without anyone knowing about it, except Dr. Curtis who was said to know about every breath people drew on the

Mission.

Sarah was twenty-one years old. A very loveable person, she was tall and slender with dark hair. As soon as Varick arrived, she wrote her family telling them that she would not be coming home for Christmas due to work commitments. She said she would be spending Christmas Day with friends and would not be home until December 29, when she would come for the New Year. Sarah's mother was a strict Salvation Army soldier who never had an inkling that her beautiful daughter would go handy to a man, let alone a tall handsome American. Her father, however, was of a different caliber, he often told his daughter to make sure she would never leave this world an old maid.

"Dees could get barred out of heaven for that, Sarah," he'd say and then he would laugh.

On the twenty-eight of December, Varick and Sarah and Cabot walked onboard the S. S. Prospero. She was helping him with his luggage.

The vessel was unloading mail and freight. They went directly to his stateroom where everything was ready to accommodate the passenger. Sarah started crying when Varick said good-bye. He assured her that he would be back as soon as the film was completed, even if he had to walk all the way on snowshoes from the nearest train. He promised he would write and let her know where he was from time to time. She told him she loved him and would be expecting to hear from him soon.

"Yes darling," he said, " I will write you every week until I get back to see you again so don't cry anymore."

He then asked Sarah if she would marry him in the summer.

She replied," Yes, darling, I will," and they kissed, a sweet, lingering kiss they both had difficulty breaking away from.

Then, looking into her lover's eyes Sarah said with great feeling, "Varick, the lamp on my bedside table will stay lit until you come back to me. I promise you, I will keep it burning day and night."

Again, he told her that he loved her and would miss her. The two of them said good-bye as the coastal boat cast off her lines, leaving Sarah standing on the wharf with tears streaming down her face, and Varick with a heavy heart as he waved good-bye to her. He kept waving until she was no more than a speck on the horizon.

Chapter Fourteen

Varick arrived back in St. John's around the eighth of January. The trip from St. Anthony to St. John's was a rough one. The weather was stormy and snow and ice covered the ship. The Prospero was storm bound for three days in Bonavista and this gave Varick the opportunity to visit three of the sealers who had been with him the previous winter when they made White Thunder. The men would be going on the Viking with him again this winter.

When Varick arrived at his office in St. John's he had a letter waiting for him from Paramount Pictures in Hollywood requesting his presence there as soon as possible. He sent a wireless advising he would be leaving for Hollywood right away on the first boat out of St. John's to New York. He also sent a wireless to Sarah telling her he was going to Hollywood on business and would wire her again on his return to New York. When he arrived in Hollywood he was immediately whisked into a meeting with the head people in movie production. They told him that the heads of Paramount Pictures had viewed the White Thunder movie and liked what they saw. However they were of the same opinion as he was. The movie needed more drama, and for this they were prepared to put up extra money to shoot more film of the seal hunt.

Varick was delighted, he knew that his old friend Robert Flaherty had been able to work on his behalf. After the meeting, Varick and Robert were invited to the executive director's office for a meeting. Jessie Lasky, the founder of Paramount Pictures Ltd. sat in a large leather chair as the two men walked in, accompanied by Lasky's secretary.

Jessie Lasky was a genius. He knew the film industry in all its aspects. He congratulated Varick for having put together the movie, White Thunder, and for directing it the way he had.

"Under the conditions out there on the ice floes, it must have been an enormous task, Varick. I admire you for your work, especially the sound outside the studio," he said.

Varick thanked him.

Lasky told Varick he looked forward to having his company, the Newfoundland and Labrador Film Company, do another movie immediately after White Thunder was finished.

Following the brief meeting, Varick went to another office where he signed the necessary papers to complete the contract to finish the movie he had started.

With the contract signed, he immediately wired Harry Sargent and Penrod, who were living in New York, asking them if they would be prepared to meet with him as soon as he got back concerning completion of White Thunder.

He quickly received a reply from Sargent telling him the two of them would be prepared to meet him as soon as he returned to New York.

When he arrived back in New York, his father informed him that he was requested to go to Montreal, Canada, to attend an International Grenfell Association (IGA) board of directors meeting immediately. Dr. Grenfell had wired him in care of his father and this kind of threw him off. He got in contact with Harry Sargent and Penrod and quickly told them what was happening.

"We plan to go back north to Newfoundland and do more shooting of the White Thunder picture and I need your help," he said. "In fact, without you I don't see how the job can be

The Day of Varick Frissell

done."

The two men agreed to go with him without any further persuasion. He asked them if they would leave immediately for St. John's, Newfoundland. They agreed and he thanked them.

After sending a wire to Sarah, he left by train for Montreal. After three days of meetings there, he left for Newfoundland.

Before proceeding any further, it is important readers know about the kind of explosives Varick was trying to obtain. As we learned earlier, the plan was to use explosives in combating icebergs in order to create drama and he had been told the explosive called thermite was on the market and available. Thermite is an explosive which, when mixed with nitroglycerin and water, will burn like nothing else. In commercial use, it is mostly used for underwater welding. Varick's plan was to melt three-inch holes about 20-30 feet into the side of icebergs, pack them full of dynamite and blasting powder, then set it off, causing the berg to flounder then roll over.

After being told this was what he needed, Varick contacted a Dr. Barnes of Montreal. While it is not known what advice this explosive specialist gave him, Barnes did tell him the head office of the explosives company was in New York City.

When Varick arrived in St. John's, Harry Sargent and Penrod were already there. They were glad to see him when he walked into the King George V Institute. The three men sat down for an all day meeting. They were surprised when Varick told them that Captain Bob Bartlett would not be going with them.

"I met with him and we talked for hours about what should be done to increase the quality of the movie. I also had a week with Dr. Grenfell in St. Anthony and had the same reaction from him as I had from Bartlett and Robert Flaherty," he said.

After Varick explained everything and pointed out what he thought the public needed to see they both agreed that what was needed was action, not acting. However, Harry Sargent was concerned that without Bartlett there would be a lack of discipline aboard the Viking. Varick convinced him that everything would be fine. During the afternoon, it was decided they would approach the Nickel Theatre to set a date for a public showing of White Thunder, maybe the first week in March because they were due to sail to the ice March 9.

But then they changed their minds and decided it would be better to have a private showing of the film with invited guests only. So, on the night of March 5,1931,Varick opened the doors of the Nickel Theatre in St. John's and had a private showing of his unfinished movie, White Thunder. It was a packed house with sealing captains from all the ships getting fitted for the hunt filling the front rows. Those fellows were anxious to see it and especially wanted to get a chance to see Captain Bob Bartlett acting out his part because they all knew him.

Every politician in the city was invited, including the Governor. However, the news media was not allowed in. Varick didn't want to take the chance of having any bad publicity about the film before it was finished. Any news here would be news in New York and he knew if some reporter gave the film a bad review there would be no chance of returning to the ice fields.

After the showing of the film, Varick and his two assistants met with about twenty of the most prominent guests. They were people who knew a lot about film quality, and had a good idea about what the public wanted. Each of them passed an opinion and it became all the more apparent that something in the film was missing. The general opinion was what Varick had said all along: More drama was needed. The story was good but without the cruel elements of the mighty ice field against man and his ship it would not become the movie they wanted it to be.

Everything was now ready to go. Most of the sealing ships had already gone to the ice with the rest heading out in the morning. It was decided the Viking would head straight for the area of the Grey Islands, depending on ice conditions.

Fred Best, from St. John's, was Varick's camera helper. He was an able man who knew what he was doing. He had been with him on the Viking the year before and had proven himself to be an excellent man for the job. Varick had told him he wanted him to work with him on any film he would be working on from now on and Fred agreed.

The general manager of Bowring's, Mr. Eric Bowring, informed Varick that there would not be a large crew going on the Viking this trip.

"The market for seal products is so low that if we weren't chartering the ship for the movie, we might not even send her out at all. She will, however, be sailing with a hundred men less then last year."

Varick, unconcerned, said, " It's not the men as much that we will be filming this time, it will be the ship and the ice."

It was clear to Captain Kean that the forecast was not so great for the next few days. He told Varick the forecast called for the wind to be northeast by north at around forty knots for twenty-four hours before switching to another direction. That night, it was decided the Viking would sail the next day.

Varick and his film crew talked about the storm the Viking would encounter after leaving St. John's. They decided it would be to their advantage to have a camera mounted somewhere on the top of the wireless shack, the highest part of the ship except for the mast. This is where wireless operator, Clayton King, spent his working days and nights. They mounted a wooden stand on the roof and had their tripod affixed to it. This would give Varick a clear view of the whole ship forward of the buildings at the mid-section and all the way back to the rear of the ship.

Captain Abram Kean, junior, the master of the Viking, was told to cooperate fully with Varick and the film crew. The charter was quite generous for the company, but he was told not to tell the sealers because they might become unhappy if the film crew wanted to go to certain areas to film icebergs where seals might not be plentiful.

Chapter Fifteen

During the afternoon of March 8, the Viking took on the explosives needed to create drama for the film. The explosives included dynamite, blasting powder and nitroglycerin. It also included flares of all description. It is thought thermite was also taken on board without many knowing about it and stored between decks amongst the food stores, because the cook's helpers were told not to smoke or light matches while down there.

What really surprised Varick was when the dynamite caps were stored with the explosives.

"My god, do any of those fellows know what they are doing, Harry?" he asked with concern, after seeing men coming aboard laden with kegs of powder and dynamite and with pipes in their mouths.

"Look, those pipes are lit because you can see the smoke coming from them," said Harry Sargent.

Varick was very concerned, and in fact almost frightened, even before they left the wharf. Harry just shook his head.

"I hope they know what they are doing," he said.

"Yes, so do I," said Varick.

He stopped one fellow and asked him if he knew anything about explosives. The fellow replied, "I only know that I can carry one keg of it at a time. They told us in there that you can throw this stuff in the stove and it won't even burn."

Varick said no more, only let the man go on.

New Yorker A.E. Penrod was one of Frissell's main cameramen. He was, in fact, the expert when it came to filming. Before Penrod left his home in New York his wife asked him if she could go with him to Newfoundland and make the trip with him on the Viking.

She said, "I am afraid to let you go on this trip, Arthur. I'm afraid something might happen to you."

He was surprised to hear her say this and told Sargent about it after they got so far into the trip. He told Sargent he'd said, "My dear, I am afraid to let you go because there is a saying among the sealing captains that if there is a woman aboard the sealing ship it is sure to bring bad luck or something terrible may happen."

With that statement, he said, she decided not to go.

Penrod's assistant was a man named Noseworthy from St. John's. Penrod couldn't believe he would be sleeping next to a dynamite magazine where all the explosives were stored.

"Listen, Varick," he said, "I'm not at all happy about this, my God, suppose an accident happened? Where do you think I would be one second later?"

Varick and Sargent didn't answer.

After a few minutes, Varick said, "Listen, the minute we get out of port we are going to move the stuff and put it somewhere else."

Penrod replied, "It should be down in the cargo hole. My God, Varick, I've never heard of anything like this before, a ton of powder and a ton of dynamite, plus all the caps. And, the crowning glory, all of that nitroglycerin thrown in on top of everything."

Penrod paused, then added, "And to make it even worse they're got it all stacked next to our sleeping quarters, dining room and saloon."

By now, Penrod was more then concerned. He said, "Why didn't Kean tell all of us that have to sleep here to each take a package of dynamite in the bunk with him, there's no difference."

"I know, I know, Penrod, I'm just as concerned about it as you and I intend to do something about it the first chance I get," said Varick.

This seemed to pacify Penrod and the men went on loading the explosives.

Sargent and his assistant, Noseworthy, sat at the dining room table onboard the Viking. They were drinking coffee and discussing how they were going to be able to mount a camera on the top of the radio shack.

"The salt spray coming over the bow will be bad," said Noseworthy.

"You're right," said Sargent, then added, "Maybe we could get some canvas and put it up in front of us, you know to kind of shield us."

Noseworthy agreed it might be a good idea. As the two men sat there talking they were disturbed by the noise of men loading cargo. Men were passing the dining room door carrying five gallons cans of something.

"What do you think is in those cans, Noseworthy?" asked Sargent.

Noseworthy paused for a moment then said, "It looks like kerosene to me."

Noseworthy stood up and walked to the door and questioned one of the men, an old guy who had a five gallon can in each hand. The man looked at Noseworthy and said, "This is kerosene in these cans, Skipper. We got a hundred cans like those to take aboard. This stuff is being stacked next to the powder and dynamite."

The old guy laughed, then added, "'Shore is a good mixture, lots of powder and kerosene."

It was obvious to the old sealer that what he was doing was not what it should be.

Harry Sargent put on his coat and stepped outside. He walked along the side of the ship toward the rear and saw where the men were stacking the five-gallon cans four high. He could smell the kerosene and knew that there must be at least one of them leaking, or maybe there were some stoppers loose. He said to one fellow, "I can smell kerosene, can't you?"

The fellow admitted that he could too.

"There must be at least one broken open or something," said Sargent.

"But that don't matter, kerosene oil won't hurt you. You can drink that stuff. The old women puts that stuff in candy when they makes them," said the man.

A couple of fellows heard the man talking to the young American cameraman and they all started laughing. Harry did not reply. He turned around and came back to the dining room. He sat down near Noseworthy and shook his head.

"What do they use that stuff for, Noseworthy?" he asked.

"They use it in the cooking stoves here on the ship. And the men take some of it with them to use if they want to boil the kettle to make tea while they're out on the ice," replied Noseworthy.

"I don't know about all this," Sargent said, "but why doesn't the captain have that stuff stored down in the hole in a safe place where it should be?"

Noseworthy knew what Sargent was trying to say.

"It's the same as what we talked about yesterday," he said, "when you get people doing whatever they please, it's amazing what you might see."

He paused, then said, "I can tell you one thing, if Captain Bob Bartlett was skipper you wouldn't see powder and dynamite stored in the toilet and next to the dining room."

Harry Sargent knew at once what Noseworthy meant. Abe Kean could not control the people onboard his ship. And for that reason, from then on, he became a worried man.

Chapter Sixteen

Clayton King was the wireless operator on the Viking during this trip. He was a fearless man. In fact, one had to be in order to stay day after day in the Marconi room, or the wireless shack as it was called.

The wireless shack was the highest room on the ship and overlooked the entire deck. It had large windows with a door facing the rear. The smoke stack was about twenty feet ahead of the shack. There was, however, no problem with the thick black smoke that billowed out of the stack at all times. The stack was so high that the smoke went back over the shack's roof.

Varick needed to send a wireless. He went to the wireless shack where King sat with the headphones tightly clamped over his ears. When he saw Varick come in and shut the door, he knew that he wanted something.

Clayton took off the headphones.

"Good day, Varick," he said.

Varick shook his hand and pleasantly said, "Good day, Clayton."

The two men talked for a few minutes then Varick asked him if he would send a wireless for him.

"Yes, I certainly will," he replied.

Varick stated the wireless. It was to Sarah at St. Anthony. Varick did not want the wireless to sound like a love letter. He just told her he was leaving St. John's and would be contacting her as the trip unfolded. He signed off, "Love, Varick."

Clayton appeared to get a kick out of doing this for Varick. He told him that anytime he wanted a wireless sent to just let him know. Clayton was from Brigus and just two days before he left home he became engaged to marry Belle with a wedding planned for the spring. His own love life made him very interested in sending wireless messages to Sarah from Varick.

King later wrote about the Viking: " The Viking! Old Adventurer of the Sea! I can still see her as she lay moored on the south side of the harbour of St. John's, ready to go."

The Viking was a relic of the days of wooden ships and iron men. She had engaged in the seal fishery for years and her staunch hull had weathered many of the sleet-laden storms of the Atlantic. On the morning of March 8, 1931, the crew of the Viking and all the sealers went to work shoveling coal into horse carts, which the horses hauled to the ship. A chute was put in place and the coal slid down into the coalbunker. By noon, enough coal had been put aboard for the trip.

A hose containing fresh water was inserted into the tanks and the water for the ship's boilers was put aboard. The crew then filled the tanks supplying drinking and cooking water.

Several trucks came in the afternoon and brought food for the voyage. It was generally what they called in Newfoundland "rough grub," especially for the sealers, including several sides of fresh, wrapped frozen beef, which were hoisted up into the rigging.

In order to cook and feed all the sealers aboard the Viking on this trip the normal galley, which was suitable for a crew of twenty, wasn't sufficient so a second one was constructed. The day before, the captain had the ship's carpenter, Mr. William Bartlett, and a group of other men build a forward galley with all the cooking facilities. This is where all the meals for the sealers would be cooked. The new facility was 8 feet by 20 feet, made of wood, and nailed to the deck of the Viking. It was built just ahead of the forward hatch.

As the crew of the Viking busied themselves with preparations for the trip to the ice fields, the remaining ships began leaving at varying intervals until all had gone. The Viking was the last ship left in the harbour going to the ice fields.

As each vessel left the harbour, Captain Kean blew the horn in salute.

"We are the last sealing ship left in the harbour, Captain," said Varick.

"Yes, I know," said Kean. "We should be ready to leave between three and four if all goes well."

"Great," said Varick, who was anxious to get going.

King wrote: "At 4 p.m. on March 8, 1931, the Viking, last of the northern fleet to leave port, swung her head for the channel."

King referred to the men onboard the Viking as happy, adventurous, heroic fellows, as much at home upon the heaving sea as on the deck of a ship. Here and there in the crowd a solemn faced, serious-minded individual might be seen, an old timer to whom the adventure had become more or less a business. But for the most part the ship was crowded with young bloods, ready in the confidence of their wonderful physique and power of endurance to foot the hazardous battle amid the crashing bergs and the crystal masses of the great white solitudes.

There was swirling gray mist along the overcast sky obscuring the hilltops on the south side of the harbour as the Viking cast off her lines from Bowring's wharf. Varick and Harry Sargent stood on the upper deck near the radio shack with their cameras going as the steam engine kicked into motion.

"Hold that hawser tight," said Captain Kean. "We'll push the stern off first, then back off and clear the wharf."

The sailor holding the heavy hawser signaled that he had heard and understood. When the ship had moved away from

The Day of Varick Frissell

the wharf all the other ships and schooners that were tied up around the harbour and not going to the seal hunt started blowing their horns as a salute to the Old Adventurer.

The Viking was a black mass as she slowly headed out in the late afternoon. It was 4 p.m. with no sun to brighten the dark grayish cast of the buildings along the waterfront.

The evening was frosty. And, some roofs were covered with snow turned a dark gray by soot from coal burning furnaces. The two men could see puffs of smoke coming up from the chimneys of the buildings all over the city and from the ships, schooners, and boats around the harbour.

When all the horns stopped blowing their customary farewell salute, the Viking blew a long farewell, three long whistle blasts, as she passed through the channel and slipped out into the cold Atlantic. One old woman on shore was heard to remark that it sounded as though the Viking was saying a final good-bye.

Cabot, Varick's Newfoundland dog, stood near his master and wagged his tail as he looked up at Cabot Tower towering high upon Signal Hill up above them. The dog had a large massive chest and powerful front legs. He wasn't a dog that would win a beauty contest but he was a faithful companion. Wherever Varick went, Cabot was there.

"Come here, Cabot boy," said Varick and the dog moved close. "Harry, turn your camera over this way, get a shot of Cabot looking at Signal Hill. Try and get Cabot Tower in the picture if you can."

"Take the dog and move over by the rail, that will give me a better angle," said Harry.

Varick walked over to the rail with Cabot.

"Hold it right there," said Harry.

Varick and Cabot stood still.

"Now, point toward the tower, and make sure the dog is looking too," ordered Harry.

"Beautiful," said Noseworthy, who was holding the tripod tight. "We should turn around now and go back because that shot should be enough to sell the movie worldwide."

They all laughed.

"No kidding, that was a great shot," said Sargent.

"Sure was," said Noseworthy.

"Let's go below for coffee," said Varick.

Sargent pulled the canvas tarp down over the camera and strapped it tight.

"I think we are in for a heavy breeze of wind from the northeast," said Captain Kean. "The weather glass is gone almost bottom up. When you see that, you can be sure we're in for something."

The Viking had not gone very far before she was into a snow squall. The land behind quickly disappeared as the heavy seas rolled down upon her.

William Kennedy was the navigator on the Viking during this trip. He had a lot of experience taking ships to the ice fields having spent twenty-four years going out in vessels of all descriptions. He had navigated ships in every crook and cranny around the coast of Newfoundland and Labrador and made two trips to the far north with Bob Bartlett. Kennedy had also made several trips to the Caribbean and the Mediterranean. He knew what he was doing.

One of the greatest things with Kennedy was that he spent all of his time in the wheelhouse with his charts. Whenever the ship was in motion, Kennedy was on the bridge. He didn't mind dealing with any captain and when he said to the wheelman, "You got your degrees to steer by and don't alter course till I give you the order to change it. Makes no difference what the captain or anyone else says," everyone knew he meant what he said.

Captain Abe Kean trusted him, and had confidence in his ability to get around on the ocean no matter what the weather conditions were like. On this cold blowy evening, Kennedy was not feeling very pleasant. For one thing, he had told the captain that he should not leave port till at least tomorrow morning.

"This old wooden tub could split in two pieces if she gets caught in a heavy rough sea for a couple of days. For the sake of waiting one more day you should hang tough," he said.

But Abe Kane was determined to get going as soon as possible. Although he didn't tell anyone, he had only one thing on his mind and that was seals.

"Look, Bill, " he said, "one day can make a lot of difference when you're looking for white coats. And besides that, the crowd from America want to get a lot of film shots of the rough seas so this should be a good chance."

Kennedy didn't answer, he knew the decision was entirely the captain's and he didn't want to interfere. The Viking would sail. Kennedy came to the bridge shortly after the ship set sail. He knew where the Viking was bound and that was around the Grey Islands-Horse Islands area. He had his orders to go there from the company. However, with the wind in from the northeast and quite a gale blowing, he knew that the ship would have to get off land as far as possible.

"We will be steering on a course northeast for about eight hours or maybe till daylight tomorrow morning, depending on the ice conditions," Kennedy had a chart in front of him and pointed this out to the captain. "After dark, we can run her at half speed especially if the wind breezes."

"I'll go along with that, Bill," said Kean.

The man at the wheel set the compass needle at northeast and the Viking started her trip north in heavy weather.

Chapter Seventeen

Varick Frissell was whistling an Irish tune that he had learned from on old guy at Goose Cove, a little town near St. Anthony. "Don't go into the kitchen, dad, Nancy's in here with a fellow…" He sat at the salon table with a pile of papers in front of him and with Cabot at his feet thumping his tail on the floor whenever he was spoken to.

The Viking was driving her nose under at almost every cast. The captain slowed the ship to about three-quarter throttle and was only moving at a snail's pace as darkness closed in on them. Harry Sargent was still worried about the explosives they had stored close to the room where he had to sleep. He just could not get any rest. He had talked to Varick and a decision was made to move the stuff as soon as they got a chance, hopefully the next day. Sargent's job was to plan the work that they were doing a day ahead. This would be done the night before unless something unusual came up.

"Penrod and Noseworthy are up in the wireless shack. They could get a few good shots of the sea coming over the bow, that is if there is not too much spray coming over her," said Sargent.

"That's what we need," said Varick.

All the running lights were on, but nothing was visible in the blinding snow that was now falling on the ship, mixed with the salty spray. In the main galley the cooks had a great evening meal prepared for the officers and the film crew. It consisted of roast beef and vegetables, with gravy. It was a bumpy evening meal. The cooks and stewards tried their best to make the meal as pleasant as possible. But the rolling and tumbling of the ship made it impossible to keep any dishes on the table. Somehow, they ate their meal with difficulty, holding on with one hand and trying to eat with the other.

Varick put Cabot in his room (the dog slept at the foot of his bunk) and shut the door. He didn't want him to get tossed around or get in some one's way and create a problem.

He spoke to Arthur Penrod and asked him if he thought he might get seasick. The forty-year old American rolled his eyes and said, "I think I was sea sick the first time I ever laid eyes on this old tub."

Varick laughed. He knew Penrod was not a sailor the first time he met him. But he was a good man to have around, a fellow who stuck with you no matter what.

The sleeping quarters for the sealers were in the head of the ship with bunk space for one hundred and ten men. They were stuffed into quarters that were just large enough for maybe twenty. The bunks were made of 2x4 rough planking nailed together with four-inch nails. Most everyone slept on boards with just a blanket under them. A few had straw mattresses they carried onboard themselves. There was no bunk that had a single man in it, some had as many as four, sleeping heads and toes.

It would be very hard, if not impossible, to even began to comprehend what it must have been like cooped up on that stormy evening onboard the Viking, especially in the head section of the ship. It must have felt like being on a bucking horse, having to hold on in order not to get tossed to the floor, or not to get your head smashed in the ceiling above.

Imagine being there without any light of any kind. The captain put the lights out up front after the men had their evening meal. The only light visible was the fire that showed itself through the cracks in the coal-burning stove that was screwed to the floor. The lighted tips of cigarettes that showed through the choking smoke that saturated the muggy air were like blinking stars in a stormy sky. Why there wasn't a fire in that area God only knows!

The sealers were almost all men who made a living fishing or logging and since they had not been fishing since October they were prone to getting seasick until they got used to the rolling of the ship, or, as they say, got their sea legs, something which could take a couple of days. From documents written about this particular voyage, it is clear there must have been total chaos below deck in the sealers' quarters that evening.

Getting the cooked food to the men up front was quite a job. The cooks bringing the food from the forward galley back of the rear hatch to the front had trouble walking on the deck due to the rough seas. The spray coming over the bow was drenching them. The snow on deck made it so slippery that the men had to walk arm in arm and sometimes crawl. There were huge breakers rolling down that made the Viking shudder when they slammed into her, almost stopping her dead in her tracks. Half of the one hundred and ten sealers were throwing up and so sick they couldn't eat. The sick men were taking turns vomiting in the five-gallon slop bucket near the smoking stove. That is, if they made it to the bucket in time.

The men that could eat ate ravenously when the food arrived. The ones too seasick to eat took their portion and put it under their bunks for later.

On board the Viking there were a few old timers, used to such conditions and sitting around as happy as birds. Some were even singing. One old timer by the name of Jerry Quinlan of Red Head Cove was helping the rest of the men get to the bucket to vomit, and if they didn't make it on time he stood by with an old dirty mop and cleaned the mess up. He would say,

"This is the job that the Blessed Master gave me and I don't mind doing it."

At around 10 p.m. the wind increased to hurricane force, but the Viking steamed on. She was moving slowly with about two thirds steam on the same bearing, which was northeast.

There were times when the bow would go completely under water washing the deck. The roar of the wind in the rigging was at times deafening. The swirling snow made visibility nil most of the time but she plunged onward. Around midnight it was obvious to the people on watch that ice was forming on the bow. Captain Kean was notified and came immediately to the bridge.

"Looks like a lot of ice forming on the deck over the sealers' quarters, captain," said Alfred Kean, who was called the second-hand on board the Viking.

"Cut the speed, Alf," said the captain.

Alf signaled down to the engine room to immediately reduce the speed to less then one quarter.

"How long have you noticed her down by the head, Alf?" he asked.

"We just noticed it."

"It's a job to see anything with all the spray and the snow coming in your eyes, Skipper," Alf said.

"What is the temperature outside?" the captain asked.

Alf was quick to reply, "It's ten below and looks like it might get cooler."

That was not very good news for Captain Kean, he knew what it meant. "We're guaranteed to get icing up in those conditions," he said.

"You're right," said the second-hand.

"Get the bo'sun up here, I want him right away," the captain said to Alfred.

Alf quickly went below. In a few minutes he returned. "Ron will be here in a minute or two, Skipper," he said.

It didn't take long for Ronald Carter to get to the wheelhouse. When he saw the captain there he knew there must be trouble of some kind.

"What is it, Skipper?" he asked.

"There's a lot of ice building up on the front deck, the weight is starting to keep her head down a little."

Through the snowdrifts and the spray coming over the bow, Carter could hardly see what was happening.

"You're going to have to get it off, Ron" said Kean, "or she's going to take a nose dive if it gets any worse."

Carter knew what the skipper was saying was true. But how would he ever be able to get the ice off in those conditions? To put men up there with axes at this time of the night and under those conditions would be suicide. Carter sized the situation up for a minute then said, "You're going to have to turn the vessel around and run with the wind in order for us to be able to do anything with it, because even at quarter speed the sea is still breaking over the bow."

The captain knew what Carter was saying was true. As they were talking, Varick came into the wheelhouse followed by Cabot.

"Good evening, gentlemen," he said, sensing something was wrong.

Not waiting for him to ask what the trouble was, Kean said, "The head of the ship is icing up. It's pretty cold outside, and of course there are mountains of sea."

Varick was quick to reply, "Yes, I can tell by the heaving of the ship and the roar of the wind."

Everyone was trying to get a better look at the head section through the window that was plastered with snow.

"With all that build-up of ice on the head, it makes it all the easier for the waves to go over her because she is lower in the water," said Kean.

No one spoke.

"So there's only one thing for us to do and that is get the ice chopped of or at least part of it, just enough to lighten her."

Carter knew it was his responsibility to get that ice off. He looked at the men standing around in the wheelhouse. "Okay," he said, "we're going to have to try and get the ice off but you're going to have to slow her right down as much as you can."

The captain agreed.

"Just a minute," said Varick. He looked at the captain then said, "If I was the captain I know what I would do."

They all looked at the young movie producer. Then the captain asked, "What would you do, Varick?"

"Captain Kean, we all know that it is almost impossible for men to get the ice off that part of the ship tonight, the risk is too great, you could lose someone overboard. Maybe in the morning, but not tonight."

They agreed and Varick continued, "You've got one hundred and ten men up there in the head of the ship. You know what that weight is. This is what I would do. I would have all the men come back to the rear of the ship until it gets light, or at least until I can see what I am doing."

They all agreed and the captain said thanks, "I'm glad you came to the bridge, we would never have thought of that would we, Bo' sun?"

Carter didn't speak nor did Varick.

Varick liked Captain Kean. Although he was an easygoing man and it appeared most of the time the Viking was out of control as far as any sort of discipline was concerned, yet he always got the job done. Carter was given the job of moving the men.

"Where will we put them, Skipper?" he asked.

"I don't care where you put them, Ron, just bring them back to the rear," he paused, then said, "you can put twenty of them in your own room if you have to."

Varick laughed as the wind outside roared.

"I am going to slow her right down, just enough to keep her up into the wind. You get ready and go up for the men."

Varick spoke up, "Skipper, I will go up and tell them if you don't mind, Carter can stay back here and get everything arranged for them."

"Okay," said Kean. "But for God's sake hold on to something, one of them waves coming over the deck could sweep you right overboard."

"I know," said Varick, as he buttoned up his heavy coat. "Put on the deck lights, that will help me see better."

It only took a minute for Varick and Cabot to reach the door of the forward forecastle from where he stepped out onto the deck. He said afterward he probably broke the hundred-yard dash. After he got to the door he found that it was locked from the inside. The men had the safety latch across. The deck under his feet was slippery. It was then that he smelled an awful stench.

"What in the world is it?" he mumbled.

He knocked hard on the door and loudly called out above the roar of the deafening wind. Cabot let out three loud barks. Someone heard them and came to the door. The man inside opened it and Varick and the dog stepped in. The men were surprised to see them but the sight of Varick and the large wet Newfoundland dog gave them confidence. There was a worried look on every face. They knew that something was not right. They had been discussing it between themselves.

"She is getting low down in the water by the head," someone would say.

Then someone else would say, "It's just your imagination, that's all."

The more experienced men who knew what was happening said between themselves, "This thing is icing up around the bow."

Varick stood and looked around as he shone his flashlight. He almost choked on the stench of vomit, and smelling tobacco smoke mixed with the foul odour. It was obvious as well that someone had been urinating in the gum bucket or on the floor. There was not enough light to really look around and see what kind of a mess was on the floor but it was so slippery he had to hold on. He heard the groans of some men as they lay in their bunks. One man said that he didn't care if he lived or died. He said he didn't care about nothing just as long as he got off this lousy crate. "What a fool I was to come out here," he groaned.

Varick silenced everybody. After all was quiet he said, "Listen men, the ship is icing up. There's no need to get alarmed, the ship is in no danger at the moment, but the captain is taking no chances."

Everyone listened silently.

"Instead of having men go out on deck in the storm using axes to get the ice off he is going to move everybody to the rear of the ship till tomorrow morning at least. This will lighten her by the head."

This was welcome news for everyone and all who could cheer did so. As he shone his light around in the darkness Varick could see that someone had emptied the gum bucket through the door onto the deck.

"Good grief," he said to himself, "what a mess."

He picked out three or four men that he knew. They helped to get everything ready for the move.

"Now men, listen," he said, "the deck is very slippery and sometimes there's a lot of sea coming over. The captain is going to slow the ship down just enough to keep up to the wind, so you will have to listen and move fast when I say the word."

They all agreed and got ready to move. Each man wore his heavy coat and rubber boots. It took about half an hour to move everybody to the rear of the ship without mishap. It was amazing what a difference the weight made to the ship after one hundred and ten bodies moved to the rear. The Viking trimmed herself, then increased her steam and moved faster through the blinding storm. It was 2 a.m. when Varick went to his room. There were four other men there. Lying on his bunk was an old man who had been suffering from seasickness all night. He was sleeping soundly when Varick walked in. The men moved as if they were going to wake him up but Varick said no.

"The wind is still picking up," he whispered quietly and the men nodded.

Varick rolled up the mat on the floor and pushed it under the bunk. At least now the men could sit in a lighted room and look at each other. Although they could not lie down, they seemed to be a little more contented.

"There are times you can't even see the light on the Binnacle for snow drift and spray," said one of the men.

"It has been like that all night," said Varick, "I was up on the bridge just before twelve and it was the same then."

Varick heard a commotion, someone talking loudly. He opened the cabin door and looked out. Men were standing in the hallway. When they saw Varick, one man said. "Stowaways, sir."

Chapter Eighteen

It must have been around 2 a.m. when King was getting ready to leave the wireless shack at the top of the ship where he had been ever since he had come on board. He had been watching the storm all night.

He saw the ice forming up around the head of the ship and suspected what was going on down on the bridge where the captain was with his officers. The ship at times was almost like a breaking rock. The sea was going over the deck, coming in on one side and out the other.

"It's all right if one of the hatches don't come off," King said to himself as he sat there watching and listening to the different Morse code messages going from ship to shore.

He finally got concerned about the ice up front and wanted to talk to someone about it. He was putting on his coat when he noticed something move near the back of the radio shack not very far from him. He looked closer... this is what he said in writing about it years later.

"As I left the radio shack to go to the cabin, I noticed two figures huddled in the lee of the shack seeking shelter."

Leaning closer he saw they were stowaways, the constant worry of all ship's masters and mates. They would smuggle themselves aboard just prior to sailing and hide among the freight or in some quiet spot. When discovered, they were the cause of masters having to turn around and take them back to port.

King went directly up to the stowaways and said, " Where did you two fellows come from?"

They were half dressed and shivering with the cold.

"Out of the stoke hole, sir," said one of them.

"Well, well," said Clayton, "you can now come along with me and see what the skipper has got to say about this."

The two came out from behind the shack.

"I can guarantee you two fellows one thing, if the captain has got to return to St. John's with you two fellows tonight, this will be one time that you will wish that you never heard talk of the Viking."

Shivering and sick, the stowaways followed King to the bridge where the Captain was.

"What in the world have you got there, Operator," asked Captain Kean.

"Stowaways, Captain," said King

"Stowaways! As sure as there's stars in the heavens," said Kean. "Well, we won't be going back for you two scamps that's for sure," he added with a tinge of anger in his voice. "But let me tell you one thing, you're going to sleep in the front forecastle with the sealers and work without pay, and when we get back to St. John's we will turn you over to the police."

Kean was a softhearted man, a fellow who never hurt anyone in his life. He was, in fact, too soft to be one of those rowdy-sealing captains in the first place.

"Now you two go down to the dining room and get something to eat and if I ever hear another sound from you while you're onboard there'll be trouble."

With that, the stowaways turned and King walked them out and turned them over to Carter.

During the night a massive wave struck the ship and rolled over the deck. For a few moments the men on the bridge thought she would never rise. The whole ship shuddered as the water slowly ran from her deck on both sides.

"What's happening, Mate?" cried the man at the wheel. The mate looked puzzled.

"Turn on the deck lights," he roared to the man on watch.

When the lights came on they saw what had happened. The newly constructed forward galley was there no more.

Clayton King wrote afterwards, "The front galley house was swept away in front of the wave and smashed as if it was an egg box."

Chapter Nineteen

Tuesday morning dawned with the terrible blizzard still raging. The wind still blew a living gale from the northeast with snow and sleet freezing on, turning the Viking into a glassy shrine. The Viking looked like a phantom ghost ship creeping through monstrous clouds in her glistening white mantle of ice. The cables coming from the cross tees high up in the mast were iced up like giant fingers reaching down to the sides of the ship as if to push it down into the boiling ocean.

The captain went below to his cabin at around 4 a.m. for a couple of hours sleep, leaving word that at the first sign of trouble he was to be called immediately.

After he left someone said, "Aren't we in trouble now?" and no one said a word.

As dawn broke and the situation was sized up, it was agreed by the crowd on the bridge there was no doubt the ice would have to be removed. And the way to do it would be getting men with axes to knock it off. However, the captain would have to make the decision to order men out on deck in this storm.

In the morning, the Viking's speed was slowed down as men were ordered out on deck with axes and ice picks. Some had sledgehammers and iron bars. Varick, Harry and Penrod volunteered to help the men get the ice off while Noseworthy and Best worked at cameras in the radio room.

The men used anything they could to knock the ice off the ship. It was very dangerous work with some men having to cling to ropes in order to stop from going over the side. It took about six hours to get most of the ice off, but the ice along the railing couldn't be touched.

At noon, the men went to the front of the ship and started working on the top of the front forecastle where everything was coated in about six inches of ice. With the sea coming over the bow, it was a frightening place to be. Even though the ship was slowed almost to a stop, the slippery conditions made the job practically impossible. But in spite of it all, the men got the job done.

While the ice was being removed, Fred Best and Noseworthy were up in the radio shack filming the whole thing.

"Now this is what you might call drama," said Best.

"Tremendous footage," said Noseworthy. "This is the kind of stuff we should have had last year, and this is what is missing from the film."

Best agreed, then said, "I can see now what Varick was talking about."

Shortly after lunch Penrod came up to the radio shack where Noseworthy and Best were with Varick and Sargent. Penrod walked in and sat down. King sat with his headphones on listening to the dots and dashes as different ships sent messages to one another. Penrod held up his hand indicating he wanted everyone's attention.

"Listen boys," he said in a voice that sounded angry, "I'm frightened."

Best was quick to answer, "The ship is in no danger, Penrod. Most of the ice is off and if the skipper runs her at half speed there shouldn't be much more ice buildup, especially with all the salt thrown around."

Penrod was wide eyed, "Listen here, Best," he said, turning toward him, "I'm not afraid of the ice or the snow, and I wouldn't care if the spars blew off her. But it's what going on down below frightens me. Down in that powder room amongst the dynamite."

"What do you mean?" asked Varick, with much concern.

Penrod now had everyone's attention.

"The men are smoking their pipes and cigarettes around the explosives, and on top of that there are containers of nitroglycerin rolling around the floor like pieces of firewood Every time the ship rolls that stuff is going from one side of her to the other."

"My great God," said Varick, putting down a roll of film he had been holding, "I should have known."

"You all know what will happen if that powder gets set off. This whole ship is going to be blown to smithereens," said Penrod, and they all nodded in agreement.

Varick immediately rushed down to see the captain on the bridge. When he had his attention he asked if he would meet with him in his room right away. Sensing the urgency, the captain agreed. When they went in the room and the captain closed the door, Varick told him what was going on.

"We're all going to be blown up if we're not careful, captain," he said.

Captain Kean didn't appear to be too concerned.

"Don't worry about that stuff, Varick," he said, "the men know what they're doing. They're careful with fire, you know, especially the sealers, they do what they're told."

"Captain, do you realize what would happen if one spark happened to get dropped into that powder? Dear God, we've got enough explosives back there to blow this ship right out of the water and you know it."

Captain Kean didn't seem to be too concerned,

"Anyway," he said, "I'm going to send the sealers back to their quarters now so they can do all the smoking they want up there."

Varick was glad to hear that, thinking it would help cut down the chance of something happening. But he wouldn't be satisfied until he had the stuff moved to one of the ship's holes and stored in a safer place.

"Listen, Captain Kean, you promised to move all the stuff to the hole and stored the minute we got out of port," he said.

"I know, I know," said Kean, sounding as though his patience was wearing thin. "Listen, Varick, as soon as we get into the ice and the sea quiet down I promise I will have the whole lot moved into the hole and stored there."

He then moved toward the door and headed back to the bridge where he ordered the men back to their living quarters in the forward forecastle. Varick, Noseworthy and Sargent went back to the room where the explosives were stored. This room was next to the one where they were sleeping and had a toilet anyone could use. They saw first hand what Penrod was talking about. There was powder all over the floor. Canisters of nitroglycerin were sliding around just as he had said. It made them worry about being caught there if it was flat calm, let alone in an eighty-mile gale on a rolling ship.

The three men gently picked up the canisters and put them in a safer place along the side of the storage room that Captain Kean and bo'sun Carter called "the magazine."

This room was where luggage was usually stored. It was a place about ten feet square with a toilet near the entrance. "This is one time I will be taking control whether Kean likes it or not," said Varick. "The minute we get in among the heavy ice this stuff is coming out of here and into the hole."

As they left the room and came outside, Best called to them, "Come here, boys, and have a look at this, look in here."

"What's in there?" asked Varick.

Best stepped into the toilet and held the door open, "Look at the dynamite that's stacked in here, just six inches from the toilet bowl, and look at the cigarette butts on the floor. Look, there are boxes full of ammunition stacked on the other side of the toilet."

Sargent started cursing, "Come on, men, let's get out of here before something happens because I'm afraid."

The night wore on with the storm as fierce as ever. The weatherglass indicated stormy weather with no change. Just before daylight the second-hand, Alfred Kean, went to the cabin and called the captain, "You better come to the bridge, Skipper," he said. "We just had a word from the chief engineer, he says the engine room is beginning to flood. Water is starting to rise on the floor. We must have a bad leak somewhere."

This was not good news for the captain. Icing up was something they could deal with, but a leaking ship was serious.

Abe Kean jumped out of bed quickly.

"Alf, go back to the bridge and try and get as much information about this as possible. Find out how quickly the water came in and anything else you can find out. I'll be there right away."

"Okay," said Alf and disappeared as Abe pulled on his clothes.

The news spread among those close to the captain and in a few minutes everyone was up and dressed. Varick and his staff were alerted.

The storm had not let up. This was Tuesday morning, still cold and blowing, and snow covering the ship except where the salt water had it washed away.

Captain Kean was in a frenzy when he came to the bridge, "What's going on?" he asked.

No one knew so no one answered.

"Something is happening that's causing the water to come in," he said. When he got no answer from anyone he asked, "Where's Ron?"

Ron Carter, the bo'sun, came into the room.

"Right here, Skipper," he said.

"Have you been talking to the chief engineer about this matter?"

"No, not yet," he replied.

"Well, what are you doing here on the bridge? Get down to the engine room and see what's going on."

Kean's eyes were bulging, he knew this was serious.

Carter quickly disappeared but it wasn't long before he returned.

"I was just talking to the chief engineer, he says there's a possibility if we can't control the water that's coming in it could be up to the furnaces in about an hour."

Kean was jumping mad with concern, he knew the seriousness of this. If the engines shut down in this storm it would be the end of them all, the ship would go sideways, then bottom up. The waves were forty feet high.

"Listen here, Carter," he said loudly, "what's going on?"

Carter knew that the captain wanted answers.

"I talked to the chief engineer and he says the inside steam operated pumps are clogged with coal sludge and they can't get them cleared out. The electrician is working at it."

This wasn't good enough for Kean. "Get the men out on deck, Carter, and man the deck pumps as fast as you can," he ordered.

Carter knew that the old man meant business.

"Yes sir," he said, as he headed for the deck.

Captain Kean slowed the Viking to a crawl, "I wonder where the water is coming in?" he asked.

He looked out through the window but it was a job to see anything. "Probably one of the covers is off the hatches, or something?" he said as he yelled for the deck light to be put on.

As the men around him tried to see out through the windows the deck lights came on. It was then that they saw the mate heading to the front of the ship.

"Where does he think he's going?" asked Kean.

One of the wheelmen came into the wheelhouse.

"The bo'sun is gone to the front to get some of the sealers to help man the pumps, I suppose, Skipper," he said.

The skipper realized this was possible.

The storm was still raging; water was coming over the deck as the vessel was just barely keeping up to the wind. Every time a large rolling wave struck, the vessel would shiver from stem to stern.

"The hatches seem to be on, Skipper," said the mate. "But it looks like there's a crack along the deck."

He pointed to a section near the left railing.

Kean grabbed a piece of rag from a chair and rubbed the steam off the window.

"How do you know that, Mate?" he said quickly.

His tone of voice let the mate know he didn't want anyone making statements they weren't sure of.

The mate looked again, "look over there where that horse pipe is. Looks like a piece of the decking is loose to me," he said, pointing in that direction.

Kean strained his eyes.

"Get down there as fast as you can and take a look at it," Kean ordered.

Varick knew leadership was going to be needed if the men manning the pumps on deck would be successful in keeping the water out of the ship. About ten men were milling around. They were dressed in rubber clothes and wearing woolen mitts and holding onto anything they could. "I'm going on deck," said Varick as he left the bridge.

Captain Kean was glad of that, he knew that Varick would get the men moving better then Carter could. Kean also knew that Frissell realized the seriousness of the boilers being flooded. It was a matter now of saving the ship.

As Varick was heading to the deck he met Penrod, "We're into a crisis," he said. "You should take Best and go to the Marconi room and get the camera going. The ship has sprung a leak and there's fear of the boilers flooding."

"My God, what's going to happen to this tub next?" Penrod asked as he called out to Best.

Varick was dressed in a long rubber coat with a sou'wester on his head, and rubber gloves on his hands.

Carter was getting the handle ready to put into the rusty old pump. It appeared to them that he didn't know very much about what he was doing.

"Do these pumps work, Carter?" Varick asked.

"I don't know," was his reply.

One of the sealers grabbed the pump handle out of Carter's hands and immediately inserted it into the shank of the rusty pump and started working it up and down. After about a dozen pumps with no water coming another sealer called out, "Get a bucket and prime the pump."

A man ran and got a large coal bucket. He went to the side of the Viking and leaned out. When the next big wave rolled near the ship he filled the bucket and came and poured it down into the pump. The man on the pump worked it furiously. In about a minute the water was coming up from the bottom of the ship as black as coal. It was obvious to Varick these men knew what they were doing.

Varick told one of the sealers to go to the captain and tell him both pumps were pumping water.

The mate and two other men did a survey of the ship's deck and found four places where it was leaking badly. One place was particularly bad. A sheet of iron bolted to the deck had come loose as a result of the pounding of the waves crashing on it in the last two days and this had made a chute for the water as it ran along the deck. Underneath were several large holes and a lot of water was going in there.

The mate sent for a few more sealers to come and give him a hand with the pumping. However they couldn't get the sheet of iron back in its proper place. The sea was too rough for them to do repairs. At one point they almost lost a man overboard. There was only one thing and that was to keep the pumps going until the storm was over.

Below decks, men were working on the steam pumps. It was obvious to the chief engineer that the pumps would have to be taken apart and cleaned out and they knew this was going to take time, at least ten hours or more.

If they were going to prevent the boilers from being flooded, keeping the water out with the pumps on deck was their only hope of saving the ship. Varick knew a lot of manpower was going to be needed to work the pumps continually. Not wanting to overstep Carter's authority he asked the bo'sun if he could go and get a few more of the sealers to help with the pumping. Carter agreed.

Varick ran for the front of the ship, but halfway there the ship suddenly dropped in a huge wave and he almost fell flat on his face. Holding onto the hatch, he waited for the ship to rise again and cast the salty spray over him. It was then that he saw Cabot tight to him, holding onto his leg with teeth like a lion. The Newfoundland dog sat glued to the deck. Varick knew that even if he wanted to jump over the side of the ship the dog wouldn't let him. Cabot was his bodyguard.

"Okay, boy, okay," he said to Cabot as the two of them ran for the forecastle door. A sealer by the name of Pat Breen was watching what was happening on deck. He stood inside with the door half open and knew what was going on when he saw the men at the pumps. He told everyone around him that the ship must be taking on water.

"However, men, don't panic, this can be taken care of," said Pat.

Everyone looked up to this able sealer. For two days now he had been caring for a lot of men who were seasick. Varick, who knew Pat personally, was glad to see him, "Uncle Pat," he said as the sealer quickly opened the door.

"Come in here quickly," Pat said to Varick and kept the door open for the dog to jump inside.

"I want four men right away to help man the pumps," Varick said.

About a hundred voices roared, "I'll go, take me."

It was obvious the men wanted to get out on deck. They were not concerned about the danger of the rolling ship or anything else out there.

"Just four," said Varick, "get your rubber clothes on and gloves if you have any."

It didn't take long for the four men to be ready.

"Be careful, lads," said Pat as the four men and Varick went out the door followed by the big dog.

Carter went back to the bridge. He knew that Varick Frissell was going to stay with the men. He went to tell the Captain that the pumps were working and water was coming out.

When Varick and the additional men arrived near the pumps it was obvious more light was needed in order to work properly.

"We need more light, men," said Varick. He looked around for Carter then asked, "Where did Carter go?"

"He's gone up to the bridge for a warm," said someone.

The rest of the sealers laughed, it appeared that Carter was not very high in their books.

"He has to get more lights for us to see what we are doing," said Varick, as he turned to one of the sealers, "I want you to go to the bridge and tell the captain that we need more light down here as soon as possible, tell him we've got a job to see what we're doing."

"Yes sir," said the sealer as he ran for the bridge.

Sargent came and asked what he could do and Varick was glad to see him.

"There's lots to do, Harry, but I want you to stay here and keep everything going. I'm going to get a couple of lights and rig up something here," He said and pointed to the wall near them.

"Okay," said Harry, then added, "it should be daylight in about an hour, we could see better then."

"I know, but Harry, a lot can happen in an hour especially out here."

"You're right," said Harry, "go and get the lights."

It didn't take long for Kean to issue orders to Carter to go and get two lights to be installed in the area where the pumps were working. The electrician came on deck but was unable to stand up due to the rolling and tumbling of the ship. He handed the tools to Varick and went inside.

Varick hung the two lights on the wall just above the pumps and tied them tight so they couldn't swing around. Now the men could see what they were doing. As daylight came, the Captain was told that the pumps were holding their own.

The water in the furnace room was still high though and Kean knew if those rusty old deck pumps gave out they would be in deep trouble. It appeared that the main steam pumps were not going to be repaired for another four or five hours.

"Where's Bartlett, the ship's carpenter?" he roared.

Someone went and got him.

When he came, Kean said to him, "We've got to fix the place where the water is going into the hole from the deck."

William Bartlett agreed.

"I'm going down on deck and have a look at the problem as soon as it gets light," he said, then disappeared to get his rubber clothes.

But by now it was light and Kean roared impatiently. "Where's Bill Bartlett? Why isn't he out on deck fixing the holes?"

"He's getting ready now, Skipper" said one of the sailors. Kean was furious. "Tell him to get out on deck now or else."

Kean was starting to panic. He knew that this was the life of his vessel. It meant whether they survived or not.

Earlier in the day, Kean had sent word up to King asking him to contact the wireless station on Belle Isle and request a bearing from the radio station there.

King informed the captain that he'd had a wireless message from a sealing vessel saying they had tried and failed to get in touch with the station.

"Finally," Clayton said, "I was advised by the operator of another vessel that bearings from the operator on Belle Isle were impossible because they had not yet rigged their summer aerial and would be unable to do it until weather permitted."

Kean was angry but kept quiet. The wind was still blowing a hurricane from the northeast.

"There can't be any ice left in the ocean," said Kean to the men standing near him on the bridge. "We should have struck the ice pack by now." He knew that if they were close to an ice pack the waves would not be as large and furious as they were.

The mate spoke up, "We haven't even seen an iceberg."

"I wonder how long more this wind is going to keep up from the northeast?" Kean asked.

The man at the wheel said, "I would say the wind will shift around to the southeast before twelve tonight."

This was not comforting news. They knew that if they got a southeaster on top of this, it could beat the wooden vessel to pieces.

Kean thought for a moment then said, "We will run in this direction all day. If there's no change by dark, then we'll turn her around one way or another and run with the wind. It will be the only chance, especially if we get the wind from the southeast."

They all agreed.

"Listen, Mate, if there's a dally in the wind anytime today, we will turn around. Make sure of that." Kean said.

Chapter Twenty

It was a long wet, cold and hard day on deck for Varick and the sealers who were manning the pumps. There were times when some men almost got washed overboard.

The men trying to fix the cracks in the deck were finding it very difficult to get to the cracks as sea was continually coming over the deck. At around three in the afternoon they gave up trying to fix the cracks and left the deck.

"We are going to have a long night, men," said Varick as he took his turn pumping.

One of the young sealers holding onto a rope nearby said, "I don't mind this, I'd rather be out here then cooped up in that stable up front. Anyone can have my bunk. At least out here you can get a gulp of fresh air once in a while."

Varick looked around and thought to himself, "Maybe later on we might be able to rig up a piece of canvas to break the sleet and salty spray coming over us." He had it in his mind to make it as comfortable as possible for the men.

At around 6 p.m. the cooks decided to take the evening meal up to the front of the ship for the sealers. The men doing this chore were called cookees and they watched the waves very carefully. After a few big ones rolled over the deck they made a dash for the front. However, they weren't as lucky this time. A huge wave struck the ship on the port bow covering the complete deck. Four cookees were carrying two large cooking boilers filled with cooked vegetables, while the other two were carrying containers filled with other food. The chilly water covered the men completely, sweeping the boilers and everything else they had out of their hands and out over the railing into the ocean. It was just by the skin of their teeth they didn't go overboard themselves.

Varick and the men working the pumps were watching and had to drop everything and help them get back to the galley. It was a terrible experience for them. They had lost the two large boilers that were used for cooking food for the one hundred and ten sealers. But the worse thing that happened to them was their close brush with death.

Just before dark there was a lull in the wind.

"There is a drop in the wind, Captain," said the man at the wheel. Kean quickly moved to the window.

"Are you sure you know what you're talking about?" he asked. The man was sure about what he had told the captain because it looked that way. Kean went to the compass then back to the window,

"By gullies, you could be right about the wind going to haul around to the south east. I just saw a squall pitch across her," he said.

Concern was rising high.

"Get the navigator up here right away," he said to the mate.

In a few minutes Bill Kennedy was on the bridge.

"Listen, Bill," said Kean, "I think the wind is changing, have a look."

Bill looked at the compass then at the drift of the wind.

"Yes," he said, "the wind is coming around from the southeast."

Kean went to the side of the bridge and looked at the barometer that hung steady on the wall.

"It's still bottom up," he said

The Day of Varick Frissell

"You know what that means," said Kennedy, "it means that we're in for a storm of southeast wind, even harder then what we have experienced. I'd say a hurricane."

Captain Kean was a worried man. It was now getting dark and he knew the Viking would not be able to take another two or three days of pounding.

"I am going to turn the ship around, men," he said. "It's now or never, so stand by."

"Just a minute" said Kennedy.

"Yes, what is it?" Kean asked

"You had better tell the men down on deck about this because a sudden roll could throw them all overboard."

Kean knew he was right.

"Go down, mate, and tell the men to get off the deck right away because I'm going to turn the ship around."

The mate rushed off.

"I hope to God you knows what you're doing, Skipper," said Kennedy with a kind of shiver in his voice.

"Yes, and I hope so too," he said as he went over to the wheel. He stopped for a moment then looked ahead.

"Tell the engineer to stand by and open her out full speed when I say the word."

Kennedy nodded he would. He spoke to the man at the wheel. "When I tell you to haul her hard to the port you do so."

"Yes, Skipper, I will," he said.

In just a few minutes the mate came back to the bridge and reported to the captain that all the men were off the deck.

Captain Abram Kean was used to rough weather. He had spent most of his life in fishing schooners bound for the Labrador, half the time fighting for his life in small vessels that should have been put through Waterloo stoves on frosty nights as firewood. He watched the waves as they rolled down onto the bow. When the third one struck, Kean roared, "Tell the engineer to give her full speed."

Kennedy gave the word, "Give her full speed ahead" and immediately the Viking jumped ahead with the full blast of her steam boilers. With this movement, Kean gave the wheelman orders.

"Turn her full to port now."

"Yes sir," was the sailor's reply as he did what the captain ordered.

All the sealers in the front of the ship thought that they had hit something. Some of them were still seasick and in their bunks, others were setting around waiting for supper to be delivered. As the ship made the sudden turn everyone came out of their bunks and onto the floor. There were bodies everywhere piled on top of each other in the narrow walkway between bunks and the long table. Some men lay still and just cursed while others scrambled and fought to get to their feet.

"We are going down," someone said.

"Let's get out of here," others cried.

The Viking was tossed around in the mighty waves. She rolled out on her side as if she would never come back. But, luck was with the old vessel. The power from the steam boilers held up and pushed the old lady back on her even keel.

The Viking was now running with the wind in a direction that only God knew where she could end up. It was pitch dark as Varick felt his way up to the bridge. Never in his wildest dreams would he ever think that any master of such a vessel would risk turning it around in such a storm.

However, he was glad that this act of insanity was completed successfully, and she was now running with the wind. At least there was no water coming over her and they would not have to pump as much.

As Varick entered the bridge, Captain Kean was smiling.

"The risk was worth it I suppose, Varick?" said Kean.

Varick was glad the captain was smiling again. The last three days had been hard on him. It seemed that every minute there was a problem.

"For a moment it looked to me like we would not be as lucky," he answered.

"I guess we had no choice," the captain said as he looked at the chart. "The wind has shifted to the southeast and it is starting to breeze, and that's why we had to get her turned around."

"I guess you did the right thing then, captain," said Varick. Kean thanked him for his reply; he was sure that Varick understood.

As the Viking ran with the wind in the rough seas, there was a pause in the activity on the bridge, a little quiet.

"If we could only get a wireless bearing from Belle Isle," said Kean.

Kennedy called the captain over to look at a chart that he had laid out on the table. The light above it was bright and this made the chart very plain to see.

Kennedy looked nervous, and Kean sensed it.

"Put a dot on the chart where you think we are now, Bill," he said.

Kennedy looked at the chart again then replied, "From where we turned around in the storm that we just came through and taking into account the way we were slowing down all the time we should be here," he said as he drew a circle on the chart far off shore.

Kean looked at it but said nothing as he left and went over to the compass. He asked the sailor who was steering the ship, "What bearing are you on now, old man?"

The sailor looked at the compass then replied, "North West, sir, the bearing that the navigator gave me."

Kean then asked again, "You're sure?" and the sailor looked at the compass again to make sure before he replied, "Yes sir, we're right dead on northwest."

"Thanks," said Kean as he moved over to the chart again. "Now listen Bill, we want to know from where you got that circle drawn on the chart where we'll end up."

He paused, "I mean, what land will we see first steering in a northwesterly direction?"

Kennedy took the ruler and laid it on the chart. He took his dividers and in a few moments had it all figured out. He drew a straight line to the land on the outside of Catalina.

"This should be the first land that we will see," he said. His voice lacked confidence although he thought they would be close.

"How long do you think it will take us to see the first showing of land, Bill?" Kean asked,

Kennedy wasn't sure.

"I don't know," he said, then added, "no one knows, we have been stopped sometimes especially when we have had trouble. We have had a hard punch ever since we left St. John's."

Kennedy looked again at the chart, "We may not be as far off as we think we are," he said then added, "we should have no problem running her till daylight."

Varick noticed that the captain looked worried.

"This ship is going to go very fast with a gale of southeast wind in her rear," Kean said.

Kennedy knew the captain knew what he was talking about. "We should run her half speed till daylight then see what happens," he said.

Varick knew that this conversation between the captain and Kennedy was based on guesswork. However there was very little he could do about it only wait and see and look on.

Captain Kean put two men up in the Marconi room, the highest point on the ship. The men were to keep a sharp lookout for land, ice and anything else that lay in the path of the Viking. He also doubled the watch on the bridge with orders that if anything looked suspicious stop the ship. The captain then went below and turned in.

There was one good thing about the ship running with the wind as far as Varick was concerned, and that was the fact there was no water coming in on the deck.

After the ship got turned around and some men got out on deck for a closer inspection it was discovered part of the hatch covering was gone. This was where the Viking was taking on most of the water in the storm.

The one steam pump that the men down below had fixed was now working and keeping the water out. But the new worry for everyone was heart wrenching: "Will we run head long into a cliff somewhere along the northeast coast of Newfoundland?"

Varick wondered aloud how Newfoundlanders could take things so easy.

"Imagine, the captain of a ship in such weather as this not knowing his location and going to bed for a few hours rest," he said to himself as he stepped into the dining room muttering "Impossible" as he shut the door.

The smell of fresh brewed coffee cheered Varick for a few moments. Sargent sat at the table holding a mug. Noseworthy sat across from him. Sargent motioned to Varick to be quiet as he shut the door. Varick looked around. Then he heard someone singing. The sound was coming from inside the galley.

An old man by the name of Harry Brown, who was the night cook, was singing on old hymn, "Let the lower lights be burning, send a gleam across the waves, some poor sinking, struggling seaman, you may rescue you may save." The words seemed very fitting for their situation.

By now, Varick was standing near the table. He looked at the open galley door. Maybe he thought he was again standing on the platform of the Metropolitan Opera House in New York singing his début. Then, forgetting all of his troubles for a moment he threw back his head and opened his mouth and started singing.

"Dark the night when sin had settled, loud the angry bellows roar, eager eyes are watching, longing for the lights along the shore. Let the lower lights be burning...."

The singing inside the galley stopped.

The only sound was the creaking timbers of the old wooden ship as she was tossed by huge waves far out in the middle of a stormy sea.

When Varick finished singing another verse of the old hymn, an elderly old man came and stood in the galley doorway, he was grinning from ear to ear. It was Harry Brown of St. John's, second cook on the Viking.

He was a well-respected old man who everyone loved to talk to. He worked hard and it seemed like he was on every working shift. He was a Sergeant Major with the Salvation Army Corps in St. John's. But he used to tell everyone, "I don't belong to no religion, only God's religion," then he would laugh.

When he saw Varick he smiled and said, "Don't stop now, Mr. Frissell, this ship needs your singing. Outside, the storm is raging, the only safe thing we've got is what's in our hearts so sing on."

Varick opened up again, "As a Mother stills her child thou can still the ocean wild..."

When he was finished singing the rest of the hymn, Harry Brown came over and shook Varick's hand and said, "Thanks my son, we needed that and may God protect us tonight."

Varick knew that the old man meant it. He then went over to the coffee jug on the stove and poured Varick a mug of black coffee.

Chapter Twenty-one

Varick, Sargent and Penrod slept in the same room with Noseworthy and Best.

Also in the room were boxes of equipment, including cameras and film. The room was crammed full. There was hardly room to turn around.

"Listen men" said Varick, "I think we are in grave danger, this ship is sailing on a suicide course."

The men thought he was talking about the explosives.

Sargent was about to comment on the powder magazine that was just a foot away on the other side of the partition from where he was standing. But Varick quickly continued,

"We are steering on a northwesterly course and no one onboard knows where we are going to end up, not even the Navigator."

The men didn't know what to think of this statement, it took them by surprise. Penrod blew out a mouthful of air and looked up at the ceiling.

"I thought I'd heard it all by now" he said as he sat down. He then added, "I suppose there's not a thing we can do about it so we might as well sit here and wait till we all get our brains beat out in some cliff along the coast of Newfoundland."

Noseworthy spoke up, "We got her made now, don't you think? A high cliff in front of us, and three tons of dynamite and black powder in the back of us. When the two of them comes together and I'm in the middle, there won't be very much left for Mary Jane." (Mary Jane was his wife).

Everyone was silent, they were too upset to smile. Then Varick said, "There is only one thing that I can tell you and that is we should all get our life jackets on. It's our only chance."

In writing about this story afterwards, Sargent said that Varick would not let him take off his life jacket or his boots for one minute during the night, or until land was seen.

Varick lay back on his bunk. For a moment he did not know what to think. His thoughts were disturbed when Cabot jumped upon the foot of his bunk and lay down.

"At least the dog is not worried," he said for everyone to hear.

He thought about Sarah and where she was at that very moment. Probably snuggled in her bed thinking about him and watching the flickering lamplight on the wall in her bedroom, the room where he would give anything to be once more. He longed for Sarah and wondered if he would ever see her again. He decided he would send her another telegram as soon as he got the chance, maybe tomorrow morning.

With all the goings on aboard the ship, he felt he was losing hope but he banished that thought from his mind.

Fred Best was so worried he couldn't stay in the room. He went out and closed the door behind him. He went to the galley where Brown was still singing and getting the evening meal ready to take up to the sealers. It would replace the food that the men had lost when the sea swept over the ship earlier. He stopped singing when he saw Best come in the galley.

"Hello Fred," he said as he walked in.

"Hello Uncle Harry," Best replied in a downhearted voice.

Harry Brown was no fool. He had been out on many ships good and bad in his day and had weathered many storms.

"That fellow Frissell can sure sing, can't he?" Brown said to Best

"Yes," said Best.

"And he knows the hymns too," said Harry Brown.

Best sat down on a stool near the table and watched as the old man took soup out of a large boiler that was on the stove.

"Varick is a worried man, Uncle Harry. I'd say that he could be grey before daylight."

Brown looked at Best then asked, "What do you mean by that, Best?"

Best knew the old man knew how to comfort everyone. He looked at him and said, "He's frightened to death, Uncle Harry and he's not the only one. We're all frightened."

Harry laid down the soup ladle and looked at Best, then asked, "Why are you all worried, Best?"

Best told Harry Brown about how the ship was on an unknown course and how scared they all were. When he finished talking, he looked at Harry who was grinning from ear to ear.

"Best, I want you to do me a favor will you?"

"Why sure, Uncle Harry" he said.

"I want you to go and get this young Varick for me if possible."

"Sure," said Best as he got up and left.

Varick and Best walked into the galley where Harry Brown was getting the food ready. When he saw Varick he greeted him warmly.

"Mr. Frissell, how are you?" he said with great respect.

Varick knew that this wise old man needed him for something important. He also knew that he had to be up front with him.

"Health wise I am fine. But mentally I am a total wreck," Varick said honestly.

"I know, I know, you are worried, I sensed it just now," said Brown.

The Day of Varick Frissell

Varick had an idea that Best had told the old cook what was going on.

"This wind is going to drop out with the rising of the sun, we are going to have a good day tomorrow, sir" said Brown. Varick looked at the old man as he started to fill up another large pot with soup.

"The reason that I'm worried is because we are steering on a course unknown to the people responsible. We may slam into the shoreline, and if this happens it could be the end of us all."

Brown put down his soup ladle and came close to Varick.

"I sent for you, Mr. Frissell, because when you were singing out there just now it let me know that you possessed something great. I'm proud that I heard you sing, especially when we are in the eye of the storm."

He went on to say, "Don't you worry, this ship is in the hands of one of the best navigators that's on the ocean today and that is Bill Kennedy. I have sailed with him for years in the worst conditions that a ship could ever be out in and he always came through."

Varick said nothing.

"You see, if Bill thought he was going to run into a shoreline tonight he would stop the ship."

Varick looked at him and saw confidence on his face.

Brown added, "Don't you worry about anything, this ship won't run ashore, not tonight."

Varick felt better, as if a load had been lifted from his shoulders.

"Would you fellows like to have a bowl of rice soup?" Brown asked.

"Yes we would, Uncle Harry," they both replied.

"Okay," he said. "After I serve you, I will round up someone to take the food up front to the men."

Varick spoke up," We will help with that job if you want us too, Uncle Harry."

This made the old man happy.

Chapter Twenty-two

It was Thursday morning.
"The wind is shifting around to the southwest, sir," said the seaman at the steering wheel.

Captain Kean had not slept much during the night. He had spent most of the time tossing and turning in his bunk with his clothes on. Kennedy was a man who could be trusted. Kean knew that. But yet he was still nervous.

He looked through a window dulled by condensation. As daylight approached and visibility became a little better he knew that it was going to clear.

Kennedy was in the chart room studying a group of islands near the headlands off Bonavista Bay.

Kean spoke to the men standing near the windows with eyes peeled.

"Your watch will soon be over, men," he said to them.

Kennedy came out to the bridge,

"Good morning, Captain," he said.

Kean heard him and replied, "It looks like a pretty good morning, Navigator"

"We're going to have a pretty good day, sir," replied Kennedy.

Kean felt good hearing this after the last four days living in what he called "hell on the ocean."

"My plan now is to run her for another ten or fifteen minutes then heave to and have a good look around, maybe size the water. That should give us a good idea where we are," said Kennedy.

Kean was glad Kennedy knew what he was doing.

At 7 a.m. Varick and the rest of his film crew sat at the table for breakfast. The steward serving the meal said the wind had dropped and it looked like it was going to be a great day.

"The sun should be out by noon, gentlemen," he said.

In a few minutes the captain came in and sat at the head of the table.

"The seas are dropping, we should see land soon," he said.

As they were talking they heard the engine slow and everyone looked at the captain.

"We are slowing down now, it's part of the plan that the navigator has in place. I think he is going to size the water."

Everyone felt good that this was happening, at least they had got through the night, safe. After breakfast, most everyone lit pipes or cigarettes. The captain talked about the ice and where he thought they should strike it.

"We are going to go into Pool's Island for a day or so to get things straightened out and try and get the deck fixed and we've got to try and build another forward galley on the deck," he said, then added, "this was part of our plan before we left St. John's, to go into Pool's Island for a day or so, and let the sealers get off the boat and have a walk around."

He then turned to Varick and Sargent and said, "I don't know how much I've got to thank you two fellows for what you did in the last two days in organizing the pump crews. As far as I'm concerned, you saved the ship," he paused then added, "all the officers think the same as I do."

Varick and Sargent thanked him and said it was part of their duty to do whatever needed to be done onboard ship.

"We're going to have to buy a full cooking fit-out for the forward galley because there wasn't a piece of cooking gear left after the sea swept it away," said the captain.

No comment was made but Sargent appeared not to be very pleased.

"Skipper," he said, looking directly at Kean.

"Yes," said Kean, sensing Sargent's worried tone of voice, "what is it?"

Sargent cleared his throat, then said, "there's no use hiding from you the fact that we're frightened to death aboard this ship, and it's not only the weather we're afraid of."

Kean appeared to be surprised about his statement.

"Why, my man, are you frightened?" There was a pause, and then Kean continued, "It appears that all is okay on board now that the storm has passed."

Sargent sensed that the captain knew what he was talking about and was just putting him on.

"I've told you before and now I am going to tell you again, the reason why we're frightened," Sargent had to control himself before he continued quietly, " Captain Kean, we are scared about the explosives stored in the washroom, good God man, can't you see what would happen if there was an explosion on board this ship. We would all be blown to kingdom come."

Sargent stood up, his fists clenched, "One of the men went out there just now and picked up a shovel full of blasting powder that ran out of the tin kegs last night when they were rolling around in what you're calling the magazine. He threw the powder over the side."

Sargent continued, "Don't you realize that almost every one of those kegs is leaking powder?"

(It is to be noted that the men who loaded the explosives later told the enquiry that as they were loading the 25-pound powder tins on board, powder was falling out of the tins onto the deck of the Viking and men were shoveling it up and throwing it overboard)

"And to make things worst, Captain," continued Sargent, " the dynamite is almost covered in blasting powder. It may seem that way to you but we are not all stupid, Captain. We fear for our lives."

(It is to be noted also that one of the principal shareholders in the Newfoundland and Labrador Film Company making White Thunder was Edgar Bowring of Bowring Brothers, owners of the Viking. Before Frissell came to Newfoundland in February, he contacted Dr. Barnes, an explosives expert in Montreal, to find out about a substance that would be effective in making icebergs founder. Barnes told Varick about thermite, a new explosive that created intense heat and would be excellent in causing large icebergs to roll over. Varick relayed this information to Edgar Bowring while he was in New York. It is also important to know that the enquiry into the Viking disaster received a report from Captain Bob Bartlett confirming that the movie company used dynamite the year before when they went to the ice to film.)

Kean got up from the table and headed for the door, but before he left he said, "When we get to Pool's Island we will do something about it."

No one spoke as he left. It wasn't long after Kean left that someone came down into the dining room and told Varick that they could see land.

"We are only about five miles off from shore," he said.

Everyone around the table was glad to hear this, it was news long overdue. At last something good was happening, or about to happen.

Chapter Twenty-three

Varick Frissell was someone who always wanted to see what was happening first hand. It was agreed before the Viking set sail that he would have the full run of the ship and could even help make some of the decisions concerning the running of the vessel. It was said by some of the Viking's officers while they were at the Horse Islands that Varick should have been running the ship.

When Varick went on deck the captain informed him that the land up ahead was South Pound Island and the small island to the right was North Pound Island.

"We are going to go further up into the bay and get into the lund of Big Pool's Island and drop our anchors," said Kean.

This was great news to Varick because at least he could get over the bout of seasickness he had for the last two days and get off a telegram to Sarah. He missed her so much that every time he closed his eyes he could see her.

"Good news, Skipper," he said.

There were heavy seas rolling until they got inside the shelter of Big Pool's Island. It was good to be in calm water again, especially with the sun shining. While the ship was steaming in the bay, Kean told Varick what Sargent had said earlier about the explosives.

"I am aware, Varick, that blasting powder is leaking out of the tin kegs. They're not fit to have on board in the first place. When we had powder in wooden kegs it was much better, at least you could bang them around."

Varick looked at Kean and said, "Captain Kean, you don't understand what all the concern is about, do you?"

"What do you mean?" asked Kean.

Varick kept calm. He had come out with a job to do, and he didn't want to fall out with Kean. However, at the moment he was not sure if the captain of the Viking had his wits about him or not. Was it possible that Captain Kean couldn't see what was going on around him?

"Captain Kean," said Varick as he turned to face the sealing captain, "Is it possible that no one has told you about what is going on down there in that magazine, I mean down there in that toilet-magazine?"

Kean looked surprised, "No" he said, "what's going on?"

"Listen, Captain Kean, that room is full of explosives and you know everything that's in there. It's a public toilet. Men are using the toilet and smoking. They're even snuffing their cigarettes out on the powder cans and on the cases of ammunition. Did you know that?"

Kean was furious. He'd never thought that men would be so crazy to do such things.

"What are they trying to do, blow us up?" he said.

"I don't know," said Varick, "for one thing there's not even a sign up on the door saying there's explosives in the toilet and no one should smoke there."

Kean quickly spoke up, "We will have to put a sign up in the toilet and make sure everyone knows there are explosives in there."

"Just a moment," said Varick, "that's not good enough, we want everything moved up to the forward hatch, that way we will be able to sleep a little more soundly."

Kean thought for a moment then replied, "That may not go over very well with the men sleeping in the forward hole. I've got the sealing crew chiefs staying up there and they may not agree."

Varick understood that, but something had to be done.

"Let's wait a couple more days. I will have Carter make a large sign and put it on the door of the toilet telling everyone to be careful until we get it all straightened out."

"Okay," said Varick, "we will give you a day or so to have the stuff moved."

Kean didn't like it but he had to agree.

Chapter Twenty-four

"We've got lots of lumber down in the hole to build back the galley, Skipper," said the bo'sun.

All of the one hundred and ten sealers onboard the Viking were on deck in the sunshine. People had their damp clothes hung out on lines trying to dry them. About twenty men were busy at the reconstruction of the front galley. The deck of the Viking was a busy place.

Varick and Sargent stood on the upper deck near the Marconi room with the camera going, getting shots of the activity around the deck.

"This is a scene that may be useful in the movie, Harry," said Varick. "Sometimes people like to look at scenes like this."

"I guess so," said Sargent.

As the two men looked out over the deck of the ship, Sargent said, "Did you talk to the skipper last night about moving the explosives somewhere else?"

Varick shut down the camera and looked at Sargent, then replied, "As far as I'm concerned the skipper has no intention to move that stuff anywhere else, in fact he doesn't have anywhere else to move it."

"What do you mean by that, Varick?" said Harry.

"For one thing he can't put it down in the forward hole because he has a group of crew chiefs living down there, and the rear hole has a lot of water running down through the deck."

That made Sargent mad.

"Listen Varick," he said. "I didn't come out here to get killed. We're sitting on a time bomb and you know it, I got a good mind to get someone to land me ashore at Pool's Island, at least I'll be safe there."

Varick knew Sargent was concerned and intended to do something about it, "Listen Harry, " he said, "I am going to put up danger signs to let everyone know that they have to be careful when they're using the toilet."

"That's not enough, Varick," said Harry. "We should tell Kean that if he doesn't move the explosives to some other part of the ship we will get off and head back to St. John's."

Varick knew that Sargent was a worried man and would not settle for anything less. "I tell you what, Harry, let's leave it for a day or so then I'll force Kean to do something about it."

Sargent agreed but said, "Look Varick, why don't we ask him to lock the door, that's the least he could do."

"I agree Harry, I'll ask him."

Sargent said nothing more. He didn't want to sound like a nagger.

Chapter Twenty-five

In the afternoon, the wind started to come around from the northwest.

"We are going to have a breeze of northwest wind," Kennedy said to Captain Kean.

"Yes, it looks that way according to the weather glass," said Kean as he looked at the barometer.

Kennedy noticed that the ship was beginning to swing around and head into the wind.

"This is not a good place with the wind northwest," said Kennedy.

"You're right," said Kean as he watched her swing around.

"I think we'll pull up anchors and head into Pool's Island. We've got to go to the store and see if we can buy some cooking gear and a few other things to replace what we lost in the storm."

"You're right," said Kennedy, "let's get her on the ball."

The mate was notified that they were going to move and he, in turn, got everyone busy preparing the ship for the short trip to Pool's Island.

The journey to Pool's Island took about an hour and Kean discovered the harbor was not yet thawed out, that it was still full of winter ice.

Kean knew what to do. He rang down to the engineer and had him give the engine full throttle because he knew with this speed the ship would push her way into the harbor ice.

The ship went into the ice for about a couple of lengths and then he stopped her. He knew that he was safe here; no wind or tide could hurt the Viking. There was no movement whatsoever.

Varick commented on how peaceful it was to be in such a beautiful place as this especially after coming in out of the terrible storm they had endured since leaving St. John's.

"You will see a lot of people coming out here in a few minutes," the captain said to Varick.

Sure enough, no sooner had the ship got settled away than people started coming out. Everyone aboard was on deck as the townspeople came alongside the Viking. It was great to see them. Captain Kean knew many people there and so did most of the crew.

Before the ship came into port it was arranged that a couple of men would go to the local shops and buy what was necessary to outfit a galley. While the men were gone shopping, many of the people from the town came aboard.

Fred Best, the camera assistant, saw a man coming out on the ice toward the ship, "I think I know that person coming out there, Varick," Best said, pointing to a tall man walking with a quick stride towards the ship.

"Who would that be, Best?" asked Varick.

"It looks like Tommy Ricketts to me," said Best.

"Tommy Ricketts, that rings a bell. Would that be V.C. Ricketts, Best?" asked Varick.

"Yes, that's just who it is," Best said quietly,

"I wonder what he is doing here at Pool's Island?"

Pool's Island was founded by a group of English fishermen in the early 1800s, but it wasn't until the early 1890s that it was settled. Two men from Seal Cove, White Bay, by the name of James and Thomas Ricketts, came and drove down their stakes. They built homes and raised families. However they

The Day of Varick Frissell

continued to have close ties with their relatives in White Bay, and continued visiting them whenever possible. The Ricketts were, and still are, people who keep the family names alive. And so it was that in 1901 when a young son of one of the relatives of Thomas and James Ricketts was born in White Bay the family called him Thomas after his uncle.

This young Thomas Ricketts became a man rather quickly. When he was fourteen years of age he was in St. John's trying to join the Newfoundland Regiment at the outbreak of the First World War and saying he was seventeen.

Someone knew the difference and he was turned down. But he stayed in St. John's, and in 1916 when he was sixteen he lied his way into the Army saying he was eighteen.

Sixteen-year-old Tommy Ricketts was soon to become V.C. Ricketts. (V.C. stands for the Victoria Cross, which is the British military's highest award for bravery). Ricketts fought in the battle of Flanders on the battlefields of France. In a special ceremony in London, England, in January 1919, the King presented him with the Victoria Cross and also the Croix de Guerre for conspicuous bravery. His acts of bravery are well documented in history.

And now, as Ricketts came aboard the Viking, Best and Varick were at the rail to meet him, with Cabot chasing at their heels.

"How are you, Tommy?" said Best.

"I'm great," Tommy replied.

"I want you to meet Varick Frissell."

Tommy laughed then said, " We've met before, I sold him some de-wormer for his Newfoundland dog, Cabot, a couple of years ago."

He patted Cabot on the head, "Good dog," he said.

The three men laughed and exchanged a few more words and Ricketts said the reason he was in Pool's Island was because his aunt was seriously ill.

"I'm looking for a ride back to St. John's on whatever is going that way," he said, " which way are you going?"

"We're going the opposite way, Tommy, we're heading toward the Horse Islands or down that way, somewhere up in White Bay."

Tommy laughed, "That's where I come from. My home is in White Bay."

As they were talking, Noseworthy and Harry Sargent came out of the dining room.

'Well, well. Look who's here," said Tommy as he held out his hand to Sargent.

Sargent got quite a surprise.

"Tommy," he shouted. "Where did you come from, what are you doing here?"

Tommy told Sargent about his aunt.

"Come in the dining room and have a mug of coffee with us," said Sargent.

"I certainly will," he replied.

Just then the captain called for Varick to come to the bridge as he wanted to talk to him.

"Okay" he said. "I'll be right up"

Varick asked Best if he would go to the top deck and cover the cameras for him and excused himself as Ricketts, Sargent and Noseworthy went into the dining room.

In the dining room, the steward served coffee to the three men. Tommy and Sargent talked about the night they had out on the town in St. John's a couple of years before when Dr. Grenfell introduced Sargent to Ricketts.

Tommy Ricketts was now in the pharmacy business in St. John's and a close friend of Grenfell, who made sure that anyone passing through the city enroute to work for him at the Grenfell Association went and introduced themselves to V.C., Ricketts. Grenfell himself was a decorated veteran of World War One who had served on the battlefields of France.

The men's conversation was centered around the making of the movie White Thunder and what they intended to do on this voyage. Sargent explained to Ricketts they were going to blast their way through the ice fields and roll over a few icebergs, using explosives. Ricketts was impressed. Then he asked about the kind of explosives that they were using. This was when Sargent started telling Ricketts about where the explosives were stored.

"I've never seen anything like it, Tommy. To tell you the truth, we are all frightened to death."

Ricketts was not too concerned at first.

He asked, "Why are you frightened?"

"I'll show you, come with me, I'll show you something."

The two men got up from the table and went to the toilet where all the explosives were stored. The toilet door was opened and Sargent stepped inside.

"To tell you the truth I am even afraid to be around here now. Look, that's blasting powder on the floor," said Sargent as he pointed it out.

He then explained what was going on, how the blasting powder was leaking out of the cans. He told him how men were smoking and using the tops of the gallon powder cans full of blasting powder for ashtrays.

Ricketts swore out loud. Then he said, "I've never seen anything like this before in my life, not even when I was on the battle fields of France. Someone has to be out of their mind to have men staying aboard this ship."

Sargent knew what Ricketts said was true.

As the two men left the toilet, or the explosives magazine as it was called, Ricketts turned and said to Sargent, "I wouldn't stay on this ship five minutes longer for any money. This is nothing but a death trap. The only thing I can say is that Captain Kean must be a mad man and I can see nothing but trouble."

He shook hands with Sargent then left.

Chapter Twenty-six

Varick decided in the late afternoon that he would have a showing of White Thunder after it got dark. It was probably the first moving picture ever shown in Pool's Island.

He borrowed a tablecloth from the steward and made a screen using two by fours to keep the cloth tight. Varick stood on the deck of the Viking in the chilly evening air as the reels filled with the scenes of the Viking turned and flashed on the screen one hundred feet away.

Everyone on board watched with eyes glued to the screen. And, as always, whenever the movie was shown in Newfoundland, everyone cheered as Captain Bob Bartlett came on the screen. It was a very enjoyable evening for everyone especially after the frightening storm that had almost torn the ship apart.

For most of the sealers, this was the first time that they had ever seen a moving picture. And it was very exciting to have the director of the movie there to tell them about it.

Chapter Twenty-seven

It was Friday morning, March 13, 1931, Captain Kean and most of his officers sat at the table with the American film crew. King, the wireless operator, was the last to join them. He told Varick that he had sent his wireless to Sarah the first thing that morning.

"She has it by now, Varick," he said with a grin.

Clayton told them he had been talking to a few of the other sealing ships out at the ice and they were reporting very few seals. One ship, the Algeriene, was in the Strait of Belle Isle. She was getting seals but they were scattered and the ice was reported loose and patchy.

"You never know," said Kean, "the seals might be inside the Grey Islands. I've seen it before. One time we killed several thousand between the Northern Grey Islands and Fox Head."

Everyone listened then he added, "It was the same kind of a year as this, lots of northeast wind almost every day."

"If the northeast wind got anything to do with it that should be a great place to go," said the mate.

"Captain Kean, I think we should stay here at Pool's Island all day," said bo'sun Carter.

The Day of Varick Frissell

Kean looked at him then asked, "why do you think we should stay here all day, Carter?"

Carter swallowed a mouthful of bread then replied, "This is Friday the thirteenth, you know. It's unlucky to leave port on Friday the thirteenth they say, and above all, its Friday, March 13. The old women used to say that all the babies born on March 13, if it fell on a Friday, would die three days later."

Kean laughed then said, "If I had to listen to all the old grannies' wrinkles that I have heard all my life I would go to bed and never get out any more."

Sargent did not think it was very funny. In fact, if he gave away to his feelings he would have Carter by the throat for ignoring his fears of what was rolling around the toilet just twenty feet away. But he kept himself under control, he knew that he was in a foreign country and didn't want to have a diplomatic racket on his hands.

Varick thought Kean had told Carter about the conversation regarding the explosives he had with him the night before, and that now Carter was just making a joke of it. However, he kept his thoughts to himself.

Kean turned to King and asked, "Have you heard anything from the Horse Islands today, Clayton?"

"No, Skipper, I haven't," said King.

"Maybe you should send a telegram and ask what the ice conditions are like around that area," said Kean.

"I sure will, just as soon as I finish my breakfast."

"Good," said Kean. "We will wait till we hear from the operator on the Horse Islands before we make any plans to leave port."

The previous night when everyone had gone to their quarters after the movie, Varick went to Captain Kean's room. He knocked, and the captain invited him in.

"What can I do for you, Varick?" he asked, sensing something wrong.

Varick let Cabot into the room and closed the door. He knew the time was come for him to lay his cards on the table.

He knew Kean was well aware of the types of explosives stored in the toilet and the conditions under which they were stored. He also knew Kean was aware of the connections the film company had with Bowring Brothers, and that Eric Bowring, the managing director of Bowrings, was a director of the Newfoundland-Labrador Film Company and a shareholder in the company.

Varick reminded Kean he was fully aware of what was put on board the Viking in the middle of the night and how the explosives were intended to be used. He said he was aware of the thermite stored below in the grocery storeroom as well.

"Listen, Captain Kean, I've got a serious problem on my hands."

"And what would that be, my man?" asked Kean, sarcastically.

"I can guarantee you one thing, Captain Kean, that if there is an accident on board this ship and someone gets hurt your head is going to roll."

Kean didn't like that. "What makes you so concerned about this matter now? I'm running this ship and so far there hasn't been a hitch. If I had listened to you fellows I would have stopped the ship out in the storm and had a crowd moving all that stuff and we would have all been killed."

"Well," said Varick. He was taken aback by what Kean had just said and the way that he had said it. He knew then that the stuff would not be moved, they would just have to put up with it.

"I'll tell you why I'm concerned," said Varick. "Harry Sargent is the key man in making this picture. And you know what Edgar and Eric Bowring told you at the meeting, and that was that the movie comes first and seals second for the simple reason that this year the company may not be able to sell one seal skin. Therefore, if Harry Sargent leaves this ship here at Pool's Island and we cannot continue making the film and have to return to St. John's someone's head is going to roll."

Kean stood up. "What does Sargent want me to do, what do he want me to do?" He repeated, " I've done everything that I can do so far. Carter says there is nothing wrong with the way the explosives are stored, it's like it always was and they have never had any trouble, so why the racket now?"

Varick looked at the skipper with blazing eyes.

Kean knew Varick was mad so he sat down, " I can't take the stuff and carry it up forward and store it in the hole up there. We talked it over with the men up front. That was the crew chiefs in the hole and they don't want it near them so what can I do?"

"For one thing, Skipper, you can go and find a lock and put on the door. That will keep everyone out."

"We could do that, I suppose," he said.

Varick looked at him as if to say, "What else do you intend to do?"

Kean rubbed his head then said. "Listen Varick, give me till tomorrow and we will decide what to do."

"Okay," said Varick, "I will give you till tomorrow to do something about it."

The captain agreed.

Just before lunch on Friday, Kean called the movie people together in the dining room and had a talk with them. He tried to assure them there was no danger of the explosives being accidentally set off. He told Sargent he could move to the forward hatch if he wanted to, with the rest of the crew chiefs.

Sargent declined, saying, "I am not part of the cattle drive, Captain, and I have no intentions of being part of it."

It was obvious now to Kean that he had a serious problem on his hands. "Okay," said Kean, "after we get out into the ice I am going to move Clayton King's wireless equipment out of the Marconi room and down to his room. He can work just as well down there as he can up above. We will then move all the explosives up there, away from everyone."

The decision seemed to please everyone for the moment, although Sargent was still suspicious because he knew full well that King was not going to move. He knew when the ship left port that would be the end of that idea.

Friday evening, Kean decided to haul out of Pool's Island. He ordered the engineers to fire up the boilers.

"We are going to go off for a distance and run up toward Fogo Island," he told the officers.

Some wanted him to stay and leave early in the morning but this was not to be. Kean was moving out.

Captain Kean blew the Viking's whistle three times as he was leaving Pool's Island. Some people on shore remarked that it looked like he was saying goodbye. This was the second time that was said in four days.

Others said, "It is Friday the thirteenth, he should stay here till tomorrow morning." But he didn't, he left.

Chapter Twenty-eight

The Viking headed out the bay toward Big Pool's Island. It was a clear evening and it looked like it was going to be a clear night. Kean was on the bridge with Kennedy.

"I want to go along by Fogo Island," Kean said.

"That should be no problem depending on the ice of course," Kennedy replied.

The Viking was streaming a large black streak of coal smoke behind her in the shadows of a dying sun.

"We will steam off northeast for seven or eight miles then we will haul her up to the northwest. This should take her just outside of the outer Wadham Islands," said Kennedy.

"Have you ever done this trip before," Kean asked the navigator.

Kennedy laughed, "Yes," he said, "many times with my eyes closed."

Kean looked pleased, "I guess I fooled that film crew down there," he said, then added, "can you imagine going to leave this ship because the powder magazine wasn't to their liking?"

Kennedy didn't comment.

Kean then added, "They won't get ashore now, that's for sure. If anyone wants to go ashore from now on they will have to do a lot of walking or swimming."

No one else there spoke. The captain sensed a coolness after he made that statement but he never asked why.

"Where is Alf?' he asked.

"The second-hand is having a mug-up, Skipper, he will be here in a few minutes. He said he wants to see you before you leave the bridge."

"Okay," Kean said, "I'll stay till he comes."

In about fifteen minutes Alfred Kean came to the bridge.

"Looks like it is going to be a pretty civil night to me, Skipper," he said.

"It looks that way," said Kean. "What do you want to talk to me about, Alf?"

"I was wondering what you wanted done if we ran into heavy ice. Do you want to be called or should we continue on the same course if it's not too heavy?"

"No," said Kean, "if you strike any ice, call me, and make sure the watches are fully alert at all times."

"Don't worry about that, Skipper," said the second-hand. Kean then left the bridge and went to his quarters.

There was still a heavy sea rolling on the outside but no wind. After the Viking left the shelter of Bonavista Bay, the sealers up front were being tossed around like cattle, and the same went for the men in the forward hole.

Although the temperature outside was below freezing most of the men came out on deck for fresh air. With the ship rolling in the heavy swell that had been kicked up by the stormy weather that blew a few days before quite a few of the man got seasick, and naturally they wanted to use a toilet.

The toilet with all the explosives stacked in it soon became a public washroom and most everyone using it had a burning cigarette in their hands.

"Who cares, I'm half dying with sea-sickness anyway," was their attitude. And you couldn't blame them. To sit on a warm toilet smoking a hot cigarette was better to them then medicine. The fear of igniting the powder on the floor never even entered in their minds.

Chapter Twenty-nine

It was a clear morning as the film crew prepared for breakfast. Varick had been up for most of the night. He heard the commotion when it started around midnight. When the sealers started using the toilet they also made quite a noise, especially every time they flushed it. And the noise that they made throwing up woke everyone. Sargent was so mad that he wouldn't speak to anyone even when he was spoken to. Best said that he was beginning to get contrary.

Just before 7 a.m. Varick went to the toilet and took a look around. When he came back, he told Noseworthy he was disgusted and fearful at what he'd seen.

"They must be trying to blow her up deliberately," he said.

"There are cigarettes butts everywhere, even over the floor. It's a good job that the powder is wet around the toilet or we would all be blown to bit by now," he said.

"Is it any wonder that Harry is mad this morning," asked Noseworthy.

Varick knew everyone sensed Sargent's state of mind, "you can't blame him, I suppose," he said.

Nothing else was said as the men went to the dining room and ate breakfast.

Sometime after 9 a.m. Clayton King sent word down to Varick asking him to come up to the wireless shack. Varick went to the shack and opened the door. When he saw Clayton smiling he knew that he had something for him.

"What is it, Clayton?" he asked

"Your beloved Sarah has sent you a wireless, my son. She wants you back at St. Anthony as soon as possible. She is love sick," King said with a laugh.

Varick took the telegram and read the wireless from Sarah. The contents made him lonely for her. He went back to his cabin and sat on the foot of his bunk with his face buried in his hands. His mind was in turmoil due to the events of the last couple of days. He would have to tell someone his thoughts. It was then he decided to write Sarah.

The vibration from the twisting propellers and the rolling of the old ship made writing difficult but he managed to put his words on paper. He figured he would give the letter to Clayton King to mail in the post office if they went ashore at Horse Islands.

March 14, 1931

Dear Sarah,

It seems like an eternity since I left you at St Anthony. The week we spent together at Christmas was the best time of my life and my hope is to come back and stay with you forever. We have been in a terrible storm for the last four days. This old ship was tossed around like a paper bag in a hurricane, but at last it appears that everything is going to be alright. My two associates, Penrod and Sargent, are not happy. They are very concerned about the storage of the explosives we have on board, and so am I. Hopefully, we will have it moved away from our sleeping quarters and stored in a safer place.

Clayton King, our wireless operator and mail clerk, has told me that he is engaged to be married as soon as he gets back to his girlfriend in Bay Roberts, which will hopefully be sometime in June. He has invited you and I to his wedding and I have accepted the invitation on behalf of us both.

There are so many things I want to tell you about things that have not gone well during this trip, however I will keep it for another time. I will just say that I love you darling and hope to see you soon.

Cabot is my guardian angel, he won't let me out of his sight for a second. Don't worry, everything will be alright.

I am sending you all of my love,
Varick

P.S. Say hi to Dr. Grenfell and John Newell for me, they are great men.

At around 10 a.m. the Viking struck heavy Arctic ice. They were about two miles off the outer Wadham Islands and heading just outside the eastern end of Fogo Island.

"We're right on course, Skipper," said Kennedy. "However, due to the ice field, we may have to start working our way around the inside end closer to Fogo Island. It appears it's open water to the westward."

Kean agreed. He then gave orders to the wheelman to alter course. In about an hour, the Viking struck open water again and proceeded on her journey in the direction of the Horse Islands. It was late Saturday evening when the Viking got into really heavy ice. Its location was approximately seventeen miles southeast off Cape John.

The ship was slowly pushing her way very cautiously through the ice with huge bellows of black smoke rising from her coal furnaces. Captain Kean stood on the bridge with Kennedy and a few more of the officers, keeping a lookout for any sharp underwater ice that would damage the ship as she pushed through. As darkness fell, it was apparent that this was the main patch of ice.

Earlier in the day, King had received a wireless from the operator on the Horse Islands saying there was a large field of ice around the Horse Islands stretching to the eastward as far as could be seen.

Kean discussed this with Varick and it was decided that the Viking would proceed on a course well outside of the islands for approximately seven or eight miles, heading in the direction of Grey Islands which were in a north easterly direction.

Before darkness fell that evening, the men on the bridge saw a couple of icebergs far ahead near the Grey Islands.

"There is no doubt, skipper, this is the place that we want to go," said Varick, pointing to the large icebergs in the distance.

"Okay," said Kean, "if that is the place where you want to go that's where we will head."

About an hour after dark a decision was made to burn down for the night. Burning down meant putting the ship into the ice with her head into the wind, leaving the engines going slowly and cutting the amount of fire in the furnaces which, in turn, lowers the amount of steam in the boilers.

"It looks like we should be into heavy ice all day tomorrow," said Kean.

"Sure looks that way," said Kennedy.

The men talked about what they would do the next day, Sunday. "We may see a few seals tomorrow," said Kean. "if we do, we will heave to and wait till Monday morning."

Saturday was not a good day for the film crew. Arthur Penrod was very upset when he saw the mess and the cigarette butts strewn around the toilet. Varick told the crew what the Captain had said about how he was going to move the wireless operator's equipment to King's room then move all the explosives up there. However, the men didn't believe it even though they agreed it was a good idea.

"King will not move his equipment out of there, Varick, you know that," said Penrod.

"Kean is only trying to put us off, he's got no intention of doing anything about it," said Best.

The Day of Varick Frissell

Penrod was standing near the rail on the upper deck near the Marconi house. He said, "I can tell you one thing I am going to do Monday morning, and that is if Kean is not moving that stuff by 9 a.m. I am going to send a wireless to the Minister of Fisheries, Clyde Lake, and report him."

Varick was surprised to hear this.

"Now Varick, listen to me," said Penrod. "You remember what Clyde told us the other night at the hotel. He said if we ever needed anything or had any kind of a problem while in Newfoundland just let him know, and right now I feel that I am in need of protection. Dear God, we are setting on the edge of a time bomb, and it's so dangerous that even V.C. Ricketts ran from this ship."

Varick knew that Penrod was determined to do it.

"Do you want me to go and tell the captain that, Arthur?"

"Yes," he said, "as soon as you can."

"Okay, I tell you what, if by tomorrow evening he hasn't started moving the stuff we will send the wireless, and we will all put our names on it."

Penrod agreed, but he still expressed his fear to Varick, because he had to wait another twenty-four hours before something would be done.

He then turned to Varick and said, "Better still, Varick, I tell you what you should tell the captain. Tell him that I am going to call all the sealers together and I am going to tell them about all the explosives on board the ship."

"Listen, Arthur, I wouldn't do that if I was you. You could start a mutiny on board this ship if they knew all about that"

"Well," said Penrod, "something had better be done Monday morning."

"Don't worry, Arthur, Kean will do something Monday morning."

🎬 Chapter Thirty

Long before dawn Sunday morning March 15, 1931, Captain Kean had the engineers fire up the furnaces.

In about an hour the sun peeked over the field of Arctic ice indicating that it was going to be a glorious day.

There was some movement around the deck as sealers awoke and came out on deck to stretch themselves and to smoke. Some urinated over the side while others looked keenly around for seals.

Before Varick and the film crew went to bed the night before, they made plans about what they would do the next day. It was decided that they would do some filming with the sealers out on the ice. The plan was to get the men out onto the ice and Varick, with Cabot, would lead them for about three miles up front of the ship.

Varick remembered that scene didn't exist on the film taken a year before. However, now that they were into fairly good ice, this would be a good opportunity to film it.

And there was still another reason why he wanted to get the film crew busy. It would take their minds off the explosives crisis tearing them apart.

At 9 a.m. with the sun in a good position the ship came upon good traveling ice. Kean stopped the ship and the crew got their things together and assembled themselves on deck. Varick told them what he wanted them to do. They were supposed to all go on the ice and move in single file over the rough ice behind him and Cabot.

"Just move along with your gaffs in your hands and your hauling ropes wrapped around your shoulders."

The men were more then welcome to be part of the motion picture being made. Although there was still a heavy swell rolling, causing the ice to shift with a grinding motion, the sealers had no problem moving swiftly across the sometimes grinding, tumbling ice field.

It was quite a sight to see Varick Frissell with Cabot leading a large group of sealers over the ice on this early morning.

Penrod and Sargent were high on the Viking's Marconi house, each with a large movie camera rolling.

Sargent said to Best, "A great shot, Best my man, a great scene out there and the lighting is perfect."

The plan was that the men would go ahead of the ship for about three miles. They were to wait there until the camera work was completed. They were supposed to string out for quite a ways. This would make the effects of the huge swells more prominent to illustrate the dangers the sealers had to contend with while working on the ice floes. As Penrod watched, he could see some of the men high on the ice while the rest were out of sight in the valleys of the swells rolling the ice.

"What a scene," said Sargent, "this is great footage."

It was noon when the Viking got the signal to move ahead to pick up the men.

Before the camera crew left the dining room early that morning they sat around talking about how the sealers would walk in single file up ahead of the Viking for about three miles while she was stopped. The question came up about how they would signal back to the ship when they were ready to be picked up.

"We will light a fire and make a big smoke," said Varick.

Then the question arose as to what they would burn to make the smoke.

"You're not ashore on the hills now," said Best.

Carter, the bo'sun, who was sitting at the table, spoke up, "Why don't you get one of them flares that was left over from last year, Varick, you can see them burning for ten miles or more, all you got to do is light one of them for a signal."

Varick looked at Carter with eyes blazing, "What do you mean, Carter," he said, "are you telling us that you've got some of these flares onboard this ship now, the ones that we had here last year?"

"Yes, I hid some away last year when we came back and brought them on board just before we sailed."

Varick was upset, "We told you last year to destroy them before we left the ship, not to take them ashore. They're too dangerous now to even handle, let alone carry on rough ice in a brin bag. Any sudden movement could set them off, you know."

Carter shrugged it off.

"We will have to deal with this matter later, Carter," said Varick.

Nothing else was said then about the flares.

It was hard going and it took the Viking a couple of hours to make the three miles.

"The ice is pretty heavy and packed together tight," said Kean.

"You're right," said the navigator, "we should keep her in a little closer to the Horse Islands, I suppose, maybe the ice is a little slacker in along there."

Kean looked at the Horse Islands in the distance.

"No," he said. " we have agreed to head for the Grey Islands area, that is where the two big icebergs are that Varick wants to get close to."

"Okay," said the navigator, "steady as she goes."

In telling the story afterwards, Sargent said during the time spent on the ice Sunday morning the men did not use any explosives, however it was apparent that they had a lot of blasting powder in blasting tins they carried in brin bags over their shoulders. These tins were about one gallon in size with a hole in the top about half an inch in diameter. This is where the powder went in, using a funnel. After the tin was filled, the men would put a piece of sticking plaster over the hole to prevent powder from running out. The tins were always supposed to be kept upright. On the Viking, there were a lot of these tins already filled with powder left over from the previous year. These tins were stacked in the public toilet next to the toilet bowl and some of the sealers used the tops of the tins for ashtrays. It was pointed out by the explosives expert at the subsequent enquiry that if a spark came near the pinhole the powder could explode.

On this Sunday morning, the main objective was to get shots of men traveling on the ice with Varick and Cabot, not using any kind of explosives.

Everyone ate a hearty meal on board the Viking at around noon. The cooks were busy as the ship rolled and worked its way butting the ice as it tried to move further toward the Grey Islands. It was hard going but it was great filming for the motion picture. There was no doubt this was the kind of footage needed to put drama into White Thunder.

Chapter Thirty-one

While researching this story, I visited an elderly gentleman and a former resident of Horse Islands by the name of Mr. Wilfred Curtis at his home in Englee, Newfoundland.

Mr. Curtis is formally from the Horse Islands and came to Englee after the Horse Islands were resettled in the 1960s.

I asked him if he could tell me anything about the incident that occurred surrounding the Viking during March 15,1931. This is some of what he had to say,

"Sunday morning we walked upon the hill just inside the houses. It was a beautiful morning, warm, no wind, with the sun blasting out of the heavens and we didn't want to go to church. Someone said there was a ship heading toward the harbor. We knew she was out there because someone saw her lights in the night, hove too. At eleven that morning, Uncle Abner, that's the fellow that reared me up, drove me to church. I was mad, you know what it was like, and we were just young fellows. Of course when we came out at around twelve thirty we all ran upon the hill again, and we could see her going head and astern butting the ice. We knew then that she was not going to come to the harbor, she was going to go on past on the outside. But she was having a hard time of it, hardly moving at all."

I asked Wilfred if he knew how far the ship was off the Horse Islands. And he said when she passed the island and went out of sight she was only five miles away.

He said someone remarked it was one of the big sealing ships from St. John's.

"Of course we learned later that this was the Viking," Wilfred said. " We could hear her engines roaring as she slammed the ice ahead and then astern. It was something to see."

The old ship butted the ice furiously all that afternoon. The film crew finally took enough film and came down out of the wireless room with the canisters of film.

They talked about the film shots they had taken and how pleased they were to have had the opportunity to do so.

"This is the right kind of ice for us to be blasting through, Varick," said Best, as the five men sat around their room waiting for the stewards to ring the bell for supper.

"It sure is the right kind of ice, there is no doubt about that," Varick replied. "Tomorrow morning if we are still in the same kind of ice we will probably talk to Captain Kean about getting some blasting going."

Sargent, who was writing something in his notebook, heard the comments. He stopped his writing and said, "Yes, I think that it will be a good idea, at least we will be able to get rid of some of that blasting powder on the floor in the toilet."

Varick knew what he meant.

Sargent went on to say, " It seems like every time the ship rolls, powder comes out of them tin kegs, you can even smell it when you walk along by the room."

Penrod agreed.

"Let's go out into the saloon and see if King is down from the wireless room. He may have the news of the day with him," said Varick.

It was obvious that Varick didn't want to hear anyone talking about the explosives again especially after having a good day on the ice. The five men went to the saloon and sat at the

The Day of Varick Frissell

table. It was a great place to have a yarn. They were only there for about a few minutes when Kean arrived.

"There you are, men," he said as he seated himself at the head of the table. "The mate and a few more of us decided that tomorrow morning if we are still in heavy ice it might be a good time to try some of that stuff you got for melting the ice, and of course get the explosives going too."

The film crew was glad to hear this. This is what they had come out here for.

"It's a great idea, in fact we were just talking about the same thing. The ice looks perfect for this kind of an operation," said Varick.

Kean agreed. "Okay," he said, "I will get Carter right after the men have supper and ask him to have seven or eight sealers start getting some more of them blasting tins ready for tomorrow morning. I would say that we need another twenty tins made up, that should give us about fifty tins loaded along with what we've got now."

Arthur Penrod, who was sitting next to Varick, spoke up. "Captain, for the love of God, tell them fellows whatever they do don't go smoking while they're handling that powder or we'll all be dead ducks."

"Don't worry about that, Penrod, those people are careful, but I'll tell Carter to tell them to be extra careful and not to go smoking while in there for their own good. They will know that anyway."

The stewards gave the call for supper. Then the film crew, the captain and some of the officers went to the dining room and sat together and had supper. The cooks had done a great job.

Chapter Thirty-two

This story, "The Day of Varick Frissell," is a tale that's full of controversy and denials.

With all the material that was and still is available, yet no one had ever attempted to tell the true story of what went on onboard the ill fated S.S. Viking on that voyage to the seal hunt in March 1931.

And now, I will set you down on a little grassy knoll on Green Island and let you listen in on a conversation between a man from the past, Varick Frissell himself, and Nicholena Leonardo, a modern young woman from New York. Varick will tell the story of what happened that frightful night of March 15, 1931:

I remember now quite well what was said that evening as we sat together having our supper, our last meal on the Viking. We talked about the film shots we had taken during the day and how they would add much to the production of the film. I knew that Sargent and Penrod were not happy at the thought they would have to sleep another night near all those explosives.

Penrod kept saying to me in private that each night he thought it would be his last one. Every time he heard the

toilet flush he would get out of bed and put on his pants, in fact he had hardly got any sleep at all since we left St. John's.

To describe Arthur right, I would have to say that he was a total wreck. As for Harry Sargent, he was not himself. He told me after we left Pool's Island that if he had known, he would never have come on the trip for any money because he was afraid every minute.

When the bo' sun, Carter that is, came to the table and sat down, the captain told him what he had just told us, and that he was going to start making explosive tins right after supper.

He said, "get seven or eight sealers and put them on the tins filling them up. There should be a couple of fellows among them used to doing this before so make sure that you get them."

Carter agreed. The captain then added, "Make enough to have a total of about fifty with what is there now and what was left from last year,"

"Okay" said Carter. Best, who was a St. John's man, knew Carter well, apparently he grew up with him, and he didn't mind telling Carter what to do.

He said, "Roland, make sure those fellows are not smoking while they're at that powder because you knows that it only takes one spark and the whole place is gone up in flames."

"Don't worry about that, Best, I'll handle everything."

"And another thing," said Best, "as they finish those tins make them carry them up to the dories and stow them in a safe place where they're supposed to be, not left in the toilet and used for ash trays like they're doing now."

Carter didn't like the last remark Best made.

"I don't think that's any of your business, Best," he said.

Best said nothing else. But he told us after Kean and Carter left that he was glad he had said it to him, at least now he knew what they were thinking.

This was Sunday evening.

There were a lot of church-going fellows on board the Viking, of all religious faiths. And being Sunday evening, some of them decided to get together and have worship.

After my good friend, Harry Brown the cook, had everything cleaned up and secured he walked out to where I was having a smoke and said, "Mr. Frissell, I am going to lock the galley door because someone took some of the bread that I had here last night and the captain wants me to keep this door locked after supper."

I told him it was a good idea if that was what was happening. He then told me that he was leaving the saloon door open for our use because we were doing a lot of work on the saloon table with film during the night. I told Harry he had nothing to worry about, we would not let anyone in the galley.

He told me he was going up to the front forecastle to have prayers with the men, and that I was welcome to come along. He said, "Maybe you could sing for the men."

I thanked him for the invitation and said to him, "I am too busy, Mr. Brown, I've got work to do."

"Okay, sir" he said and left.

BUT, IF I HAD ONLY GONE!

Around seven, the sealers who were loading the cans arrived. Carter was not there. Penrod got concerned about what they were doing so he went out where they were. When he came back he said, "We're all going to be blown to bits."

Some of the men were smoking their pipes.

Penrod made a statement to me, "Varick, these fellows are handling that blasting powder the same as if it was salt water, they've even got their pipes lit and are joking and laughing as if they were on a picnic."

I knew they were only going to be there for about two or three hours, so I told Arthur to be quiet, that everything would be all right.

At about 8 p.m. Captain Kean came into the saloon where we were working on the film and said that he had just given orders to the mate to get the ship in position and prepare to burn down for the night. He went on to say that it looked like there were patches of open water up ahead.

"The mate is going to turn the ship head up into the wind and put her into the ice and then burn down."

"Great idea," I said

Penrod brought out all the rolls of film that they had taken that day and placed them on the table. For a moment he forgot about what was going on next door in the magazine/toilet. His mind was centered on the films. Harry sat across from him working on the plans for the coming week.

There was a funny thing going on as far as having the right people filling the powder tins with the blasting powder. For instance, on board the Viking there was a man by the name of William Johnston. Mr. Johnston had spent twenty-four years going to the seal hunt. He was now on the Viking as a master watch with a certificate and had lots of experience using explosives. He had been very concerned with the situation regarding the storage of powder in the toilet. I had talked to him several times. This was his first year on the Viking and he didn't like what he saw and said so.

He tried to get information from Carter about what was stored in the toilet but Carter wouldn't tell him anything. He then went to the mate and asked him if he could tell him about the amount of explosives on board the ship.

The mate, Alfred Kean, told him there was around a ton and a half of blasting powder and about 700 or 800 pounds of fine powder on board. As for the dynamite and the rest of the stuff, he would have to go see the captain,

Johnston told the mate that he was responsible for forty men and he was very concerned about what he saw going on in the public toilet. But even with all the experience William Johnston had with making those explosives he was not called to supervise the men working with the explosives that evening. In fact we, the film crew, were surprised he was not with the men.

At about 8:30 p.m. the ship started slowing down.

Captain Kean came down and told us that he was going to retire for the night and that the ship was now headed into the light westerly wind that was blowing.

I asked him what our position was and he said, "We are about eight or ten miles east of the Horse Islands."

That would be just past the island and off about eight miles.

After that, he went to his room. Sargent and Penrod came in. The two of them were wide-eyed.

"We are sick and tired of talking about the danger out there in the toilet, Varick. Look, the least you can do is make a sign and put it on the door. If that was done these fellows might stop smoking."

"Okay," I said, "get me a piece of cardboard."

As Sargent went to get the cardboard, Carter came into the dining room. When I saw him, I remembered the flares he was talking about earlier that day.

"Oh yes," I said, "Carter, where are those flares you said you had?"

"What flares?" asked Carter, as if pretending that he didn't know what I was talking about.

"The ones that you said I should take today to light as a signal on the ice."

Carter said nothing and I asked him again where they were.

"Oh, the flares," he said

"I want them, Carter, now," I said.

He got up from the settee and went into the captain's room. We heard the captain talking to him as he came out of the room. What they were saying I don't know. In his hands he was carrying two flares. They were about three feet long and two inches in diameter. Sargent started swearing.

"What have you got there, Carter?" he almost screamed.

Carter immediately put the flares on the table.

"That's two flares left over from last year, Harry, I kept them to run a few experiments when we get out on the ice."

"Now you listen to me, Carter, do you know that they are very dangerous, any small sudden movement at all could set them off."

Carter didn't seem too concerned about it.

I told him to take the two flares and go out and throw them over the side of the ship because they were too dangerous to keep aboard.

"No," he said, "I'm not going to throw them overboard, I am going to keep them and when we get out on the ice I am going to run an experiment with them."

"Don't you dare," I said.

With that, Carter picked up the flares and went outside.

Arthur Penrod came into the saloon with a piece of cardboard and handed it to me.

"Okay," I said, "I will make the sign."

I put the cardboard on the table and started writing down the words DANGER.... I said, "I am not an artist but I've got to make this sign."

I had three words written down when all of a sudden the ship gave a huge roll. For a moment we all thought that she was going to roll completely over. Everything on the table fell onto the floor. We heard dishes crashing onto the galley floor, chairs were tipping over backwards. The stove near where the doctor was sitting capsized onto the floor. Everyone stood up, speechless.

Immediately the captain bolted from his room in his slippers calling out, "What's going on, what's going on?" as he ran.

No one spoke because we didn't know. He leaped up the stairs to the bridge. We sat down holding on to the table as if waiting for another roll.

Just then I heard a hissing sound from the hallway in toward Carter's room. "My God," I cried.

Wilfred Curtis in telling the story to me says that they were all in church on the Horse Islands and it was around 9 p.m.

He said, "Uncle Abner wouldn't let me come out of church till he was ready. You know what Uncle Abner was like for church. He wanted to see the key turned in the door then. And Earl, I didn't like that. You know what it was like when you were a young fellow.

"But, we were sitting there, I don't know now what was being said for sure, but anyway, all of a sudden sling she goes. The older people got a bigger fright then we did. They thought that it was the end of the world. Someone roared out, "An earthquake.

"The mantles on the lamps shook so much that they broke. With that, we all ran for the door. We were too frightened to look around when we got out. We thought we might fall into a big hole or something might grab us. Well of course, everyone ran to his or her house. But someone saw the light in the sky off to the east up over the hill."

Lot Ropson was living in Duggings Cove on the western side of White Bay on March 15, 1931.

It was 9.01p.m.on this cold winter Sunday evening and he was walking to his home with his wife when she saw a bright flash far out on the ocean, miles away.

"Something is on fire out there, Lot," she said.

Lot looked out to sea and saw it.

The two of them stood there and watched spellbound.

Then they heard a terrific explosion from over on the other side of the bay near the Horse Islands.

"Something is blown up for sure, maybe the Germans is attacking us again," his wife said.

Lot, being a humorous kind of person, said, "Maybe the

Horse Islands fellows is attacking the Germans out near the Horse Islands."

"Don't go joking about that, Lot, someone may be hurt out there right now, you know."

Bob Ropson of Roddickton, Lot's grandson, told me that story while I was doing research. He said that his grandfather and his father talked about it for years. They said it was the sealing ship Viking. Bob said the remains of the Viking's hull drifted ashore near Dugging's Cove and settled on bottom near the shore.

"It was a bright flash that I saw and it struck me square in the face, and I thought that it had torn my head off," said Varick, as he stood with his hands over his face.

It was obvious to Nicholena that he was crying.

She walked over to him and put her arms around him and said, "Don't cry Varick, just tell your story."

He dried his tears then hugged her, then continued with his story.

Cabot was lying down on the floor near my feet when the blast hit me. It appeared that the whole housing section of the ship lifted off. Then another explosion followed this one. This caused a terrible fire and also lifted the back of the ship. I felt something across my legs that wouldn't let me get up. The flame was so bright that I couldn't see anything. That must have been the thermite stored down below that was on fire. Then I saw someone near me. It was Clayton King. I noticed that the mizzenmast was down across both of our legs. We were caught and held by the legs. Then another explosion sounded and I pulled my legs out from under the piece of mast. I then lifted the piece of wood off Clayton and reached over to Cabot. He was on fire. I put out the fire on his back and he started howling loudly. There was another person there but I don't know

who it was. The fire was too bright for me to see anything. It might have been the doctor.

I looked around and Clayton King was gone. I hoped he made it out alive. I tried to stand but I couldn't. It appeared that my legs were broken. I had blood streaming down my face. And as I lay there near Cabot the events of the whole week came to me like a flash. We were all expecting something to happen. Something terrible I suppose. Then it happened, and I suppose it killed us all.

I cried to Cabot to run, "Run Cabot run," I said, but the dog, my dearest faithful friend, wouldn't leave me. Then I saw Sarah. She was reaching for me, but couldn't reach me. She was crying and calling my name and telling me that she loved me. That's all I knew until I came to.

I knew that I was on the edge of a pan of ice just clear of the ship. I tried to stand up but my legs wouldn't hold me up. They were crushed. I stood part of the way up, and then I saw a man coming towards me. It was John Young, the food inspector, but he couldn't reach me because the heat was too great. That was when I tumbled headlong into the water. The cool water felt good after all the heat from the fire. I remember being in the water between pinnacle pans of ice. I was off the ship and in the water.

Cabot was pulling me through the open leads of water. And oh how warm it felt! I felt so relaxed, so comfortable, I just wanted to stay there forever!

John Young was from St. John's and he had signed on as food inspector aboard the Viking. He had met Varick Frissel the year before, in 1930, when they were making the first part of the film and they became friends. After the Viking blew up and he had retired, a reporter from the Evening Telegram in St. John's interviewed Young and this is what he said: "I knew Varick Frissell even before I joined the ship and I was probably the last person to see him alive. I saw Frissell near the stern of the ship on the ice three or four minutes after the explosion.

He was bent forward and trying to stand up. There were a couple of people near him but I couldn't recognize them. I tried to get to him but I couldn't. In less than a minute he was gone and I never saw him again, he probably fell into the water."

Chapter Thirty-three

Clayton King wrote an article about his experience on board the Viking during that terrible night of the explosion. He told the story to different newsmen and they wrote about it this way:

The saloon table ran thwart-ship along the after-side of the saloon. Carter, the bo' sun, seated himself on the after-side forward end. Varick Frissell was on the starboard side, forward end. I seated myself on his right, with Harry Sargent next. Dr. Roche, the ship's surgeon, was standing in the doorway of his stateroom, which was located on the port side of the saloon, opposite the mess-table. The navigator, Captain Kennedy, was standing by the stove, forward and was filling his pipe for a smoke before turning in.

The pride of the ship, Cabot, a great Newfoundland dog, owned by Mr. Frissell, curled himself up at our feet. Whenever Varick spoke, Cabot would thump his tail on the floor.

In his stateroom, Captain Kean was preparing to turn in for the night.

I noticed that Mr. Frissell was working on a piece of cardboard.

"Well, Varick," I said, "what are you doing?"

"Writing out notices, Clayton, warning notices."

"Why?"

"Going to post them about the ship regarding the explosives aboard, it's getting mighty dangerous around here now."

I glanced over his shoulder and read the words "NOTICE, DANGER," and the unfinished word "POW…"

What's the idea?" I asked.

"Well," said Varick, "if we are not careful the boys coming down the companion way, carrying lighted cigarettes, might cause an explosion and kill us all. As you know, we have plenty of explosives onboard."

As he finished speaking, Varick, as if struck by an after thought, turned towards Carter,

"While I think of it, Carter, where are those old flares stored that you told me about this morning?"

"In the skipper's state room, in a locker under his bunk," Carter replied.

"Bring them out to me immediately," Varick said.

"They're a serious menace if kept there, they could explode with very little movement."

Carter entered the captain's room and returned shortly with the flares in question.

"Say, Sargent, give me a Lucky will you?" said Carter.

Sargent passed the cigarette, but Carter didn't light it as far as I know.

"Carter," said Mr. Frissell, "those flares are damaged, and are not safe to keep aboard. Better take them out and throw them over the side immediately, destroy them."

"I'll keep them and make some experiments on the ice tomorrow," said Carter.

"Don't you dare! Do this. Throw them overboard, I tell you. If you fool around with them we'll be blown to Hades before daylight."

Carter picked up the flares and left the saloon, going toward his room, which was on the after starboard side of the saloon. The magazine and the toilet were located in a small corridor directly opposite Carter's room.

Dynamite and blasting powder were both stored in these rooms along with cases of termite, a highly explosive substance made up of Iron III Oxide and aluminum powder that burns at between 2000-3000C.

A few seconds after Carter's departure, the ship gave a terrific lurch and listed over to an angle of about forty degrees.

In an instant, all was chaos. All hands were thrown clear of the mess table. The stove capsized, and Dr. Roche was knocked to the floor.

The ship righted herself almost immediately. Captain Kean came running out of his stateroom and headed for the bridge to determine the cause of the racket.

Getting to our feet we started to clean up the saloon. Then, almost immediately there followed a terrific blast from the after-end of the saloon.

For me there followed----OBLIVION.

Chapter Thirty-four

Down in the forecastle, if anyone had looked in before the explosion, the gleam of the electric lights would have shown tier after tier of bunks filled with sleeping men. Tired out after days of storm and hardship, they slept peacefully, not knowing the dangers that threatened them.

Down below in the engine room Murphy, the chief engineer, who was on watch, was going about his work, checking the auxiliaries, oiling and watching the slow turning of the shaft.

Atop the grating over the engine room, Ted Carnell, second engineer, sat reading an adventure story, completely absorbed in his magazine, little knowing that in a few seconds he would be heading for that "greatest of all adventures in the sky."

Suddenly, the old Viking shuddered and rolled over onto her side. Men were catapulted from their bunks.

Slowly the ship righted herself and lay quiet. The air was vibrant with the knowledge of the presence of danger as the fires started. Men half awake waited expectantly.

Then! A cruel, roaring, booming blast shattered their lives! Hell broke loose. "Fire! Fire!! We're on fire," they tried to scream.

Then another explosion, greater then the first, tore the ship apart. This explosion turned the forecastle into a red-hot inferno. This created a group of savage, disordered, fighting men grasping for the ladder that led to the deck.

Then there was the third explosion that brought the deck down on their heads!

Men were dying and screaming down below. White flames and showers of sparks were raging through the entire ship.

Up in the forecastle, planking was falling and pinning men to the floor, breaking bones and burning flesh.

Some men had been blown out through the sides of the ship. They lay dying on the ice, crying in the burning pain. Others were caught in the crackling, roaring flames that beat upon their ears drums like sledgehammers on smitten steel.

One of the firemen by the name of Patrick Breen escaped with his life when he was blown across the forecastle.

For a moment he could not think clearly. Then as he got to his feet he taught about his co-workers trapped down below in the engine room. He realized that he was their only hope of getting out alive. He had a deep gash in his side that was oozing blood, but disregarding that injury he painfully crawled along the burning deck until he came to a hole. Somehow he got in through it and started working his way down into the engine room. He was working his way along the engine room when he heard a cry! "Help! Help me!!!! Is there anyone up there? I'm trapped here below!!! My God is there anyone up there? Please help me."

Pat heard these cries for help coming from down below in the engine room. He looked down and it resembled the flames of hell. He tried several times to get down but was just not able to get pieces of heavy timber out of the way to get through. Finally, flames that were white-hot forced him out and he had to abandon any attempt of trying to rescue the screaming man.

Drums of kerosene oil were bursting open with the intense heat and the liquid fluid was running down into the furnace room making the fire more intense.

Pat fought his way back to the burning deck and safety.

"As for me," King went on to say while telling the story. "On regaining consciousness, I found myself on the floor of the saloon. I was dazed, unable to think clearly. I even found myself wondering what had happened. I wondered if everyone but myself had been killed. All around me everything was burning and I was face down on the floor. I tried to get up but was unable to at first. Then, as my mind cleared I knew that if I didn't move fast I would be burned to death. So I had a choice. To get out immediately or be burned to death!

I turned over with great difficulty. I noticed that there was a large piece of heavy timber across my legs. All of a sudden someone lifted the timber off. When I looked I saw a man, he was all in flames, just like a living torch.

"God, I have to get out of here," I said.

As I tried to stand I realized my two legs were broken.

"I heard the sound of something running, I thought it was water, but it was blood running from a cut on the side of my head, blood was also pouring down my face. The redness of my blood appeared to intensify in the white glare of the flames."

Clayton then started to pray, "God help me to get out of this." He prayed again, "I don't want to go down with the ship. Help me! Please help me," he cried.

"I thought of my mother and father. My clothing and my hair were on fire, and burning. Oh God help me! I cried again."

King made another effort to stand but fell back on the floor choking and gasping for breath.

"I again called on God for help and he answered me, he gave me the strength in my arms-strength that I never had, to pull myself along the floor of the saloon and out of the inferno!"

When King got out onto the deck and out of the flames he put his hands to his head and his hair came off in handfuls.

He beat at his clothes also with his hands and put the fire out. Burning them badly. King said, "The will to live is great. Life is sweet even at the worst of times."

Chapter Thirty-five

The following is how Clayton King, the faithful wireless operator on the Viking, explained what he did

"Explosion after explosion racked the ship. I crawled through rolls of films, unexploded sticks of dynamite, exploding rifle shells and kegs of powder. I pulled myself along and reached what was left of the stern of the ship. Then, I threw my legs out over the side. I had the strength of a dozen men in my hands and arms, and regardless of whatever I was going to have to face I was not going to burn to death."

As Clayton's bleeding and burned body hung on the edge of the burning ship, the bitter cold wind of the cruel North Atlantic was like a balm to his battered soul as his lungs took in the chilly frosty air. As he looked around, there was nothing but wreckage in every direction. The part of the ship where Clayton was hanging was blown away almost level to the water's edge.

"The ice was aglow from the flames of the burning ship. I heard the voices of men crying for help everywhere. Though my eyes were blurred and hazy yet on one of the ice pans not far from me I saw a man standing in a crimson pool of blood, it was gushing from a gash in his head."

"Who are you?" Clayton cried.

"I'm Kennedy," he cried. "Come out and get me whoever you are."

"I can't make it, my two legs are smashed" Clayton answered, "They can't be that bad or you wouldn't be where you are," he cried.

"My God," Clayton said, "is this then navigator?"

"Yes it's me, the navigator, who are you?" Kennedy asked in a quivering voice.

Just then another explosion shattered the hull and a body came hurling from the wreckage twisting and turning in the air. The body landed on an ice pan not far from Kennedy. The head of the man was almost completely split in two. The body was still for a moment then after a few convulsive movements, it slid off the ice pan and disappeared into the depths of the cold Atlantic.

"The heat was so great where I was hanging on," said Clayton, "that as I put up my hands to my neck I could feel the cords tightening. I knew I had to get clear or be burned. I don't remember whether I jumped or I fell, all I know is that I landed in the water between two pans of ice. I reached out and tried to get a grip on the ice but it was too slippery. There was nothing to hold on to. But faith was with me as I was struggling to try and hold onto the edge of an ice pan. Then, a set of steel hands grabbed me, and lifted me out. I'll never forget it as long as I live. It was Harry Sargent!"

Chapter Thirty-six

Harry Sargent heard Varick when he said, "Look, what's that?" and he looked towards the hallway where Carter had gone carrying the flares in his hand. It was only moments later the ship gave a heavy roll and for a moment it appeared that she was going to roll over. Sargent looked, following Varick's eyes towards the hallway just as the sudden explosion occurred. He could only remember the booming impact of the force that struck him. He knew he struck something as he was flying through the air and landed on an ice pan about two hundred feet behind the rear of the ship. He was badly shaken up.

Sargent said he immediately heard another explosion and saw the whole housing section of the ship rise up from the deck. The two sides were blown out almost down to the water's edge. The wind from the explosion was so strong it threw him backwards on the ice. Immediately, he saw huge white flames shoot into the night sky. The flames were so bright he couldn't watch them. He knew exactly what it was. It must have been the thermite that was on fire. It had to be.

He knew about the drums of kerosene stacked along the rear railing, and saw some of them when they burst open, causing flames to leap into the air. Although he was two hundred feet away he could feel the air being sucked towards the burning ship. He saw men jumping from the burning ship covered in flames. Sargent knew he was seriously injured. He had a pain in his back and his arm was hurting severely.

"I've got to get closer to the ship and try and pull some of these men out of the water," he said, as he ran toward the side of the ship.

Heat drove him back. He ran on the loose ice toward the rear of the ship. It was then that he saw a man staggering, then fall. He apparently got blown out through the side of the ship. Sargent ran over to him and pulled him farther away from the scorching heat. When he rolled him over he was shocked to discover that it was Kennedy the navigator.

"Harry," said Kennedy "where did you come from?"

It was obvious the navigator was in shock. He had a large gash on his head and was bleeding badly.

"You stay here and don't move," ordered Sargent. He looked around and saw other people jumping from the railing of the ship and hoped that he could get close enough to pull someone out of the freezing water. As he left to go towards the ship he saw Kennedy stand up and start walking toward the rear of the vessel. Sargent ran to save someone but it was too late. He then looked for Captain Kennedy and saw him standing on an ice pan close to the ship's stern. He was looking up as if talking to someone. Then he saw a man sitting on the edge of the ship close to the water. Staggering. Sargent rushed toward them. Before he got to Kennedy the man jumped. Sargent went to where the man disappeared in the water and waited for him to come up. As he broke water he grabbed him and pulled him out. "My God," he said, "it's you, Clayton."

King gasped and said, "Harry." Sargent pulled King over near the navigator. It was only then that their agony filled journey began.

Chapter Thirty-seven

Nicholena was crying as she watched the tall, handsome American standing in the sunlight. He also had tears running down his face. She moved closer to him in an effort to comfort him.

"Go on," she urged him, "tell your story, Varick."
He got himself together again and started with trembling lips.

"I felt myself being moved through the warm water. Cabot was pulling me farther and farther away. "Good dog, good dog," I said as he swam with me.
All that I could do was float around in the water amongst the ice after I had been tumbled into it. I felt so comfortable and warm. I can remember looking up and seeing a light over us, but not very far over us. It seemed to stay there.
Then I heard Sarah calling. "Varick. My darling Varick. Where are you? I'm calling out to you, Varick, can you hear me?"
"Yes, Sarah, I can hear you, I am all right, and I am so warm here with Cabot in this warm and wonderful place."
I heard Sarah call again. "Varick! If you don't come

back to me it will be the end of me, I'll die. I'll die of a broken heart. I'm alone here at St. Anthony. I can see you now. Is there anything wrong Varick? You look as if you are surrounded by big fluffy clouds?"

Sarah started crying. "Look Varick, can you see the lamplight? I still have it burning. You're getting closer. Keep coming."

Varick started crying and covering his face.

"I heard Sarah calling to me again," he said. "She said, "Look up Varick, can you see me? I am not very far from you, I am above you." I looked up at my darling Sarah and said, "I'm coming, Sarah, I'm coming. It was the last time I saw her as she vanished. And so did the light."

Chapter Thirty-eight

After Harry Sargent pulled King out of the water and onto a pan of ice, he said to him, "Don't move till I come back and get you."

Sargent then ran for about fifty feet as Captain Kennedy was about to fall into the water. Sargent lifted him up and carried him across a few pans of ice to a larger pan. King could see them clearly in the light of the burning ship. King's eyes hurt every time he glanced at the fire because it was so bright.

"It seemed as though it took less then a minute and Harry was back to me again," said King. "He reached down and grabbed me under the arms, and lifted me up."

"Put me down Harry," King said. "I can't stand any more, just leave me here. It was then that he picked me up, saying we can't stay here it's too close to the ship."

"I don't care, let me die," said King.

"Sargent jumped from pan to pan with me in his giant arms," King said, adding that what Sargent did was nothing short of heroic.

"We're to close to the burning ship, if she goes she will take us down with her with the suction," said King, whose legs were dangling. He thought he heard bones scrunching as Sargent carried him over to where Kennedy was lying.

"My good God," Sargent said. "It finally happened, I knew that it was going to happen, I knew that we were all going to get blown up"

Kennedy and King didn't speak as they watched the burning ship.

"I wonder where Varick, Arthur and the boys are," screamed Sargent over the roar of the fire.

Captain Kennedy then got to his feet. "Do you feel good enough to walk, Captain?" Sargent asked.

"Yes," was his reply.

Sargent pointed over towards the ship and to where the ice was littered with wreckage. Sargent and Kennedy walked over to the scattered debris and picked up some clothes lying there. One of them found an overcoat and put it on, the other put on a windbreaker. Up until then they were in their shirtsleeves. The ice was littered with bits and pieces of just about everything that was on board the ship. There were cans of goods and pieces of cabin doors and fittings and personal belongings of those on board were scattered everywhere.

The three men stood there with disbelieving eyes. As they watched they heard more explosions. As the fire got deeper into the bottom of the ship, things would explode and send more debris flying through the air and scattering it everywhere.

The Viking's deck was burning savagely, sending huge clouds of black smoke into the air. The men watched as drums of kerosene oil exploded, sending flames sky high.

"Listen," said Sargent, "do you hear that?" The three men stood as though frozen. "It's Cabot barking! Listen, he's still on the ship."

King could not hear the dog but Kennedy could.

"I wonder if Varick and Penrod got out?"

Sargent was wild on the ice and for a moment it looked as if he was going to rush into the burning inferno.

"They may have gotten out on the other side of the ship," said Kennedy.

Smoke and flames were belching from the Viking, white and blood red flames running up into the rigging. It seemed that the very cables were burning. The ship looked like a huge fireworks, sparks and streaks of flame raced through the blackness of the night. Men on fire were falling over the side into the water. The ship was moving away as if the propeller was still moving.

"The night was so much ablaze with the brightness of the fire that the whole world must have know about it," King told a reporter afterwards.

He went on to tell another reporter that the blaze of light, screaming cries for help, smell of burning flesh and the roar of the explosions from the shattered Viking, branded his life forever. The Viking, still in flames, slowly drifted away, or was it the three men who drifted away from the ship and out from the heat of the flames.

As they got further from the flames they realized that this was a cold winter's night. The fire they had just come through didn't affect the temperature that struck them now.

King could not stand. His injury was so great that he thought he would not last very long.

Sargent started looking around for anything that they could use to survive.

He told Kennedy they had better collect everything they could because in a few minutes the light from the burning ship would be out of range and they wouldn't be able to see to collect the things that were there.

King said that as the fire flared up again, maybe from another drum of kerosene exploding, he saw a dory nearby.

"I pulled myself over the ice with my bare hands and got to the dory," he said. "As I reached it a voice said to me, "you're saved now, Clayton." I reached up and pulled myself in over the gunwale and cried in pain as I fell into it."

King heard Sargent say. "Get all the pieces of wood that you can find, Captain. We are going to have to light a fire if we're to survive."

"I felt secure as I lay in the bottom of the dory," King said later. "I knew that the suction of the ship would not be able to pull me down now, it seemed that this was my greatest fear. As I lay there I was sheltered from the piercing wind. The burns on my head and hands were paining even worse then my broken legs."

As King lay there in the dory he felt it move. He forced himself to stretch far enough up to look out over the edge and noticed that the dory was attached to the ship by a line. And as the Viking moved away it was pulling the dory with it. King tried to untie the line but it was fouled in the smashed end of the dory and he could not get it undone.

"Lord, I am worse off here in this dory then I would be on the ice," he said, then shouted, "Sargent, Sargent, help me out of this dory. It's smashed up and attached to the ship. I am going to get pulled under."

Sargent yelled back and told King that he was going to be all right.

"My whole body was completely numb with the cold that was gripping everyone," King told a reporter.

Then, while hauling himself out of the dory he caught the flesh of his broken leg in a jagged nail sticking out of the smashed dory and tore a gash in his thigh. King howled in pain. He wondered if he would ever be able to walk again.

" Sargent left us and ran toward the burning ship with no regard for his own life. He pulled someone out of the water onto the ice, they had been yelling for help. He then went to where someone was on the ice and too close to the fire, picked the man up and carried him farther away from the intense heat.

Sargent finally came back to where Kennedy and I were. He noticed a portion of the ship's stern that had been blown away and was sitting on a pan of ice. He knew that this would be the safest place for us, for a while at least, depending on the movement of the ice in the rolling swells.

Sargent and Captain Kennedy started to make plans about what they would do, because they were fully aware that this was where they were going to have to stay with me because of my broken legs. It would be impossible to move me. I knew that Captain Kennedy and Harry Sargent would never walk away and leave me.

Captain Kennedy and Sargent were wondering why more of the crew had not shown up. By this time we were drifting farther from the ship. It was impossible for Sargent to get back to the men he had rescued due to leads of water that had opened up.

They figured that most of the men had struck out for the Horse Islands, and there is no doubt that the two would have done the same only for not leaving me. If they had left and started for the shore they would have saved themselves a lot of untold suffering and possibly Captain Kennedy his life," King later said with tears running down his face.

Sargent then found some old rags that were lying around and, doing the best that he could, bandaged the cuts on the heads of King and Captain Kennedy.

Chapter Thirty-nine

The news of the Viking explosion reached St. John's early Monday morning. The whole colony of Newfoundland became abuzz with this tragic news. Many questions were asked, "Why, and how did it happen?" being the first question. Then, "I wonder did anyone get hurt?"

The Viking was a famous sealing ship. Over the many years that she had been out to the seal hunt with thousands of men serving on her, there had never been anyone killed on her before. But now people waited anxiously for news of the explosion, would it be possible that everyone had escaped.

It took half a day to get a ship ready to go to the rescue. The first news to reach the outside world came from the wireless operator on Horse Islands. It was to the Minister of Fisheries and read,

Horse Islands
March 16th, 1931
To, the Minister of Marine and Fisheries.
St. Johns, Newfoundland.
At nine o'clock last night heard terrible explosion. Early this morning, the burning wreckage of a steamer Was sighted about eight miles east of here.

Also saw men traveling on the ice toward Horse Islands.
There are no particulars about incident as yet.
(sign) Otis Bartlett
Operator Horse Islands.

The Minister of Fisheries, Clyde Lake, took control of the rescue operation. He immediately ordered all ships that were at the seal hunt to proceed to the Horse Islands area without delay. He ordered Otis Bartlett to stay at the wireless office on Horse Islands until the crisis was over. He then ordered ships that were at St. John's to proceed to the Horse Islands for possible rescue.

The oceangoing tug, Foundation Franklin, and the S.S. Sagona were at once prepared for the trip. The Franklin took Dr. Blacker and several nurses aboard and left. The Sagona played a greater role, as Lake ordered all the necessary rescue equipment and supplies put aboard the vessel. The ship took foodstuffs, medical supplies and three doctors: Patterson, Moores and Martin as well as nurses Paton and Rose Berrigan. Clothing for the survivors was also put on board.

The ship left at 6 p.m. on Tuesday, March 17. Captain Jacob Kean was the skipper and he, along with a full crew and a team of fifty volunteers, steamed at full speed towards the disaster area.

Chapter Forty

Clayton King, Harry Sargent and Captain Kennedy were sitting in the center of a pile of debris, which was part of the rear section of the Viking. They were drifting on the ice floes of the frozen Labrador Sea.

Sargent was worried sick about Varick Frissell and Penrod. He doubted if they were as lucky as he was. The sound of Cabot barking in the midst of the fire was not a good sign, because he knew that the dog would not leave Varick there. If the dog was in the fire, Varick was there also. But he kept hoping against hope that they had made it safely out.

When they established their surroundings, Sargent and Kennedy decided what they would do.

"We have to get a fire going, Captain," said Sargent.

The captain agreed, then said, "Imagine, a little while ago we were running from the enemy fire and now we need it to survive."

Sargent said, "We live in a strange world, even this is like a nightmare."

"Life is a nightmare, Harry," said Kennedy.

Their thoughts again were centered on the fire that they had to get going.

"I have a lighter here, Captain," said Sargent.

Kennedy had a pocketknife in his pocket but was unable to get it out because he was shivering too much.

Sargent noticed and took the knife out of his pocket for him. It was apparent that hypothermia was setting in due to the cold, the captain needed warmth, and fast.

And fast it was. Sargent was a tremendous outdoorsman. He had spent a lot of time in the wilderness around North West River, Labrador, in company with Varick.

He took the pocketknife and pieces of the split wood and some of the debris and in a few minutes he made shavings and had the fire going.

The pan of ice that they were on was only rubble made from frozen winter slob. Sargent gathered every scrap of the wreckage that he could find and tried to build a shelter for King, at least he could be sheltered from the howling wind that was now beginning to pick up.

As the night wore on, Sargent and Kennedy kept the fire going with pieces of wood from the stern section and anything else that would burn. The temperature that night was probably minus 25C, taking into account the wind chill factor.

Sometime after midnight, the wind came up from the northwest and blew a heavy gale. There were times when snowdrifts made visibility zero. King said the grinding ice and roaring wind almost burst their eardrums.

During the night as he lay there, King wondered about the events of the last week. The terrible storms they had encountered. And, how the battered hull of the Viking withstood the pounding of the heavy seas no one would ever know. But most of all he thought about the times that Varick and Penrod went to Captain Kean and complained about the danger of the blasting powder and explosives stored in the toilet. They begged and cried for him to do something about it, but to no avail. He had seen with his own eyes all the powder strewn over the floor and the large kegs with powder spewing out.

"If only the captain would have listened," King said aloud.

The hours dragged by like years as the three men drifted with the pack ice. Finally dawn came and the sun came up.

"It's going to be a clear day, I think," said Kennedy.

"I hope so," said Sargent.

"As I lay there," King said later, " Sargent came and knelt down by me and looked at the fractures of my legs. One of my legs was smashed so bad the shin bone was sticking out through my pants for about five inches."

King's other leg was also smashed in several places below the knee and was turned up towards his body but there were no bones protruding. He had lost a lot of blood and was very weak. Sargent said later he knew if King wasn't kept warm he would not last very long, and for this reason he fought to keep the fire going.

Sargent noticed that Kennedy was becoming very pale.

"Are you all right?" he asked.

Kennedy knew he was beginning to get sick, "I'll be all right, Harry, it's not me that we've got to worry about, it's King here with the broken legs."

Sargent said nothing else.

As the morning wore on the sun shone its glare onto the ice that reflected into the eyes of the three men, causing them to be snow-blind.

King said that the bright glare of the sun shining on the blue white ice was like sand thrown into your eyes. Whenever you blinked it was like a sandpaper effect, very painful.

At around noon, Captain Kennedy noted they were drifting fast to the southwest and pointing his hand in a westerly direction he asked, "Do you see that point of land over there, Sargent?"

Sargent looked, shading his eyes, "Yes I can see it," he said.

"Well, that's Cape John, if we keep on drifting in this direction we will go into Notre Dame Bay. If we get closer someone might spy us from one of the communities there."

"It was a glimmer of hope to hear him say that," said King.

As they drifted, each man thought about what his destiny

was going to be. Clayton wondered if he would ever walk again even if he did get rescued. His two legs were smashed and if he had to lose them, what use would he be to himself or anyone else? For a moment, he lost all hope and thought it would be better if he never got rescued. He wondered if his dear Belle would ever marry him.

While researching this story I went to see the great Frank Mercer. He is great because he was one of the renowned Newfoundland Rangers who policed the colony of Newfoundland in the 1930s and 1940s, serving both on the island of Newfoundland and in Labrador. I asked Frank if he knew anything about the Varick Frissell story and this 87-year-old distinguished gentleman invited me into his house and sat me down in his den.

"I know it all," he said, "all about the Viking disaster. What would you like to know?"

I asked him if he knew anything about Clayton King, the wireless operator. He told me everything about him both before the Viking disaster and after he came back. He started by saying that he came close to being on the Viking himself, as a stowaway.

"Only for my mother I would have been aboard," he said.

I asked him how and he replied, "The Viking came in here to Bay Roberts to pick up a crowd of sealers and I was going to go aboard her and hide away but mom found out about it and stopped me."

He then went on to say that Clayton had a girl friend who lived next door to his family and a few days before the Viking came to Bay Roberts to pick up the sealers Clayton got engaged to her.

"They were going to be married sometime that summer," he said. "I heard mother talking about it. After he lost his legs in the explosion he spent a long time in the hospital. His girl left and went to the mainland and never came back."

Frank was silent for a few minutes then said, "She was a wonderful person but I guess the thought of marrying a man with two legs gone was too much for her."

Frank said after the girl's father died he bought all of the family land from her.

Out on the ice, meanwhile, Sargent thought about Varick, Penrod and Best. Would he ever see them again? He hoped they hadn't burned to death. That would be a terrible death to die, he thought. They were continually on his mind. Every time he looked in the direction of the burning wreck of the Viking and saw the smoke he just had to banish the thought of Varick from his mind.

As Kennedy stared with watery eyes, he wondered if his navigating days were over, would he ever see the narrows of St. John's again? He too seemed to lose hope.

The hopelessness and the thoughts of last night were causing their nerves to become strained. Several times during the day Sargent would jump to his feet and yell out that he saw a ship coming, however, this would turn out to be nothing but low clouds along the horizon.

"Monday afternoon I started to slip into unconsciousness," King recalled later. "When Sargent would arouse me into consciousness again, the realization that this was the end would almost drive me out of my mind. Many times I would slide down close to the water's edge and Sargent would have to pull me in closer to the center of the pan. Captain Kennedy was beginning to get sick. "Get me a drink of water, Sargent, will you," I pleaded in my semi-consciousness state.

"Wait for a few minutes and I'll melt some snow," said Sargent, as he held up a can he had picked up among the scattered debris that had probably come out of the garbage.

As I started to drink the water out of the can I felt a burning pain in my face and knew that it must be the same as a piece of cooked meat.

Late Monday evening there were heavy clouds in the western sky. Captain Kennedy surveyed the sky for sign of weather.

The Day of Varick Frissell

"If it rains tonight boys, we're all finished for sure," he said.

Sargent knew the captain was right. It would be a miracle if they survived the night in dry clothes, let alone in wet ones.

Kennedy was sitting down near King watching the horizon while Sargent stood and scanned it continuously. Darkness settled in on the three men as the wind picked up.

"We have got to get a flag ready just in case a ship happen to come in sight," said Sargent. "A flag waving can be spotted farther away then something not moving."

"There are two or three flags over there," said Kennedy. Sargent saw them and went and picked up what are called sealers panning flags. He found a stick about six feet long, tied the flag to it, and stuck it up.

Sargent, in telling his story to a reporter in New York, said King went into a coma shortly after dark.

"For one thing I was glad that he did because he was suffering so much. King was lying amongst some rubble that we had gathered, with a few pieces of broken timber belonging to the stern of the Viking. Captain Kennedy was having trouble sitting up."

"Just before daylight I heard Sargent screaming," King later said. "He grabbed me and started shaking me and saying, "Wake up, Clayton! wake up." I could not answer him for a moment then I heard him almost screaming, "God! Oh God! What am I going to do? King is dead and Kennedy is dying! I'm finished." I don't know how long Sargent had been shaking me before I came to my senses. He was saying, "Wake up Clayton, wake up or you'll be finished."

King opened his eyes and said, "I can hear you Harry, but I'm freezing to death." Sargent moved King closer to the fire. King went into a coma again just before noon on Tuesday.

Captain Kennedy was awake and sitting up.

"How do you feel now, Captain?" asked Sargent.

"'I've got a terrible headache and I'm freezing to death."

"I'm afraid to build the fire too big, we've got to spare our wood because we don't know how long we may have to be here before someone rescues us."

"I know," said Kennedy in a disheartened tone.

Sargent noticed that the captain was breathing heavily, indicating he was getting a cold on his chest.

King lay near the small fire, wrapped in a few old rags that Sargent and Kennedy had found scattered round.

Sargent looked at his broken legs. "What a mess," he said. "I wonder if he will survive. It looks to me like his two feet are frozen solid. What pain he must have."

Kennedy also looked at them and agreed with Sargent that King's two feet was indeed frozen.

"If something doesn't come along soon, Captain, I don't hold out much hope for him."

"If something doesn't come along soon I don't hold out much hope for any of us," said the captain.

Sergeant stood up and scanned the horizon. It was getting late. He looked at his pocket watch, then at the sun.

"If we have to spend another night here I don't know what we will do," said Sargent.

Kennedy was worried. There were times when he could just barely sit up.

"We've got no guarantee of ever getting rescued," said the captain.

Sargent stared at him then asked, "What do you mean by that, Captain?"

"There may not be anyone looking for us yet."

"Why," asked Sargent.

"My man, no one might even know yet that we blew up, unless they saw the fire or heard the explosion."

Sargent's heart sank.

"Do you know if there is a wireless station on the Horse Islands, Captain?"

"I'm not sure, but I think there is," said Kennedy.

"King knows all about that for sure," said Sargent.

With that, he reached over to King and gently shook him.

"Clayton, Clayton wake up. Can you hear me?" King did not come awake. "Clayton." he called again, but no response.

Sargent started shaking him and calling his name.

King opened his eyes and said, "What is it Harry?"

"Do you know if there is a wireless station on the Horse Islands? Come on, wake up."

"Yes, there is" King answered quickly.

"Are you sure, Clayton?"

King rolled his eyes then said, "Yes, there is a station on the island. The name of the operator is Otis Bartlett. I was communicating with him on Saturday"

Sargent asked King another question, but King closed his eyes and he had to shake him again to get his attention.

"Does St. John's know the station is there?"

Kennedy spoke up, "You knows they know that there is a wireless office on Horse Islands, the government owns them all."

"I'm not talking about the government, captain, I'm talking about Bowring's, they may not know about the office up there," said Sargent.

"Yes they do, they knows about every one that is in Newfoundland," said Kennedy.

Sargent shook King again and asked, "Did you tell the wireless operator we were coming to the Horse Islands area?"

"Yes, I said that we would be in the Grey Islands area sometime Sunday, depending on the ice conditions."

Sargent and Kennedy were glad to hear this. There would be no doubt that if anyone saw or heard the explosions they would report on it for sure, thought the two men.

Captain Kennedy was a very quiet kind of man. Maybe this was the reason he was not the master of a sealing vessel. "He knew too much and he was too quiet," was what people said about him. Kennedy spent his summers as captain on the Petrol, a government fisheries patrol vessel.

Sargent was aware that Captain Kennedy knew about all the complaining that the film crew had done about the storage of the explosives. And how they had begged Captain Kean and the Bo'sun to do something about it, but to no avail.

"Do you remember Friday evening just before we left Pool's Island when Carter wanted Kean not to leave, that it was bad luck to leave port on March, Friday the thirteenth, and he wouldn't listen. Tell me something, Captain," said Sargent, "why didn't Kean listen to us when we went to him time after time and told him about what was going on in that toilet?"

Captain Kennedy was freezing to death and breathing heavily, and it appeared even then that he would not live another hour. But with all of that, he was not prepared to say anything about the captain of the Viking to the young American standing near him, even as the sun was going down for another terrible night, maybe his last.

"Someday the reason may come out, Harry," said Kennedy. He paused then added, "If the right questions are asked."

Sargent said nothing else about it, he was only concerned now with how they would survive another night.

Chapter Forty-one

The coastal ship Sagona, a former sealing vessel and one of the best icebreakers the colony had, was dispatched from St. John's to look for survivors from the Viking.

The Sagona struck a storm after leaving St. John's. The captain did not slow down. He plowed on through at full speed with every eye on board watching. The vessel struck strings of rough ice around the Funk Islands at 8 a.m. but it was only strings, however it made the sea smoother.

By mid-afternoon, the Sagona was in the vicinity of Gull Island off Cape John, and steaming through fairly heavy ice.

Captain Jacob Kean stopped his ship and called everyone together and had a brief meeting.

"Now men," he said, "you are here for one thing and that is to look for anything that is not ice. It's a good day for seeing things. Report anything you see and everything that you think you see. From what we have figured out here, and with the wind direction that the Horse Islands wireless station has reported, we should see something in this area."

Jacob then went on to tell them, "I want every man to station themselves around the sides of the ship and keep your eyes wide open and report everything." They all agreed.

The next morning, before the sun was up, it appeared to Sargent that his two comrades were either dead or would never be revived from the coma they were in, especially King.

During the night he warmed water from snow and gave some to them both. Captain Kennedy was beginning to cough a lot and you could hear every breath that he drew.

Sargent opened a can of beans they had found near the explosion and warmed it by the fire. He offered some to Kennedy, but he refused saying that he would have some later. Around noon he decided that he would have to shake King again to try and get some life in him. It took about half an hour to get him awake, but finally he did it.

"Where do you think we are now, Harry?" King asked.

"We're close to the Newfoundland Hotel," Sargent joked. Even in the state he was in King smiled, then asked, "Do you think that we will ever see the Newfoundland Hotel again, Harry?"

Sargent said later, while telling the story, that he was encouraged by that smile of Clayton's. He gave the two men some more warm water and moved them closer to the small fire. Sargent said every time he looked at King's broken and frozen legs his heart ached and tears filled his eyes because there was nothing he could do for him.

Chapter Forty-two

Early on the morning of March 16, an old minister went to the door of Mr. Roland MacKean in Boston and asked to see his wife, Alma, the sister of Harry Sargent. Knowing that he was on business, Alma invited him into the parlour. He immediately told her that he had bad news about an explosion aboard the sealing vessel Viking that was out amongst the Arctic ice floes with her brother, Harry, aboard. He told her there was no news about the condition of anyone in particular, only that there were people unaccounted for and that her brother was among them. For a moment Alma was shaken, however she knew that Harry was a tough man and if there was anyone who could survive on the Arctic ice it was him. She asked if there was any news of Varick Frissell and was told he was also missing.

The minister then took the wireless from Newfoundland and read it to her: Sorry to inform you that your brother, Harry Sargent, who is listed as an explorer aboard the sealing vessel Viking and is also part of the film crew with Paramount Pictures is missing after an explosion around 9 p.m. Sunday near Horse Islands, Newfoundland. Every ship at our disposal has been dispatched to the area. We will keep you informed.

The message was signed by H.B. Lake, Minister of Marine

and Fisheries, Colony of Newfoundland.

Alma immediately boarded the passenger ship, Silvia, and headed to St. John's, Newfoundland.

Out on the ice, Harry thought about his sister. He knew that if he didn't live to get out of this situation it would also be the death of her because they were so close. Although she was happily married to a fine man, yet she was in contact with Harry everyday, when possible. After their mother's death she became his guardian angel and wanted to know his every move.

A reporter by the name of T.M. McGrath sent a special cable to the New York Times when this crisis was unfolding. He said Henry Sargent in his prime was a magnificent specimen. He was six feet six inches tall and as strong as an ox. He was rough and tough and would tackle almost anything.

But here was Harry now, helpless in a field of white ice in freezing weather, with two dying or dead men with him.

"What can I do?" he asked himself over and over again but got no answers.

Going over to Clayton he put his ear next to his mouth and listened for his breathing. He was relieved when he heard air going in and out of his lungs, but the sound was very faint. It was then that Sargent noticed something on the ice near King. It was an envelope. He realized it must have fallen out of King's pocket as he writhed there in pain during the night. Sargent reached down and picked the envelope up. Although it was soaked in water the address was still very plain to see. It was the letter that Varick had written to Sarah the day before, and Clayton had intended to post it at the first opportunity. The water had unsealed the envelope. Sargent opened it and took out the letter. It was still readable. It was written with pencil and he immediately recognized Varick's handwriting. It started with "Dear Sarah" and ended with "don't worry, everything will be all right."

He knew this was Varick's last letter, that is, if he never got out of the Viking alive.

He wondered what he should do with it, whether to keep it or throw it away.

Sargent folded the letter and put it back in Clayton's pocket. He then put his hands over his face and wept. The letter was never seen again.

Sitting next to King, Sargent lifted his upper body up and pulled him into his lap, pulling the old heavy soggy coat he was wrapped in up over him. He wept as he looked at him and held him in his arms. He thought about King's mother and father whom he had never met, only heard King calling out to them when he thought he was at the point of death.

King lay there for about ten minutes and started to blink his eyes and stir a little. Harry thought he heard him faintly talking, "Darling, darling, don't leave me, please don't leave me. I'll be home soon."

He knew that King must be dreaming about the girl he was engaged to marry when he got back. Harry held him for more than an hour then laid him down on the cold Arctic ice. He had no choice. He stood up again on the highest part of the ice near them and surveyed the horizon but saw nothing.

Several times during the morning, Sargent thought he saw a ship, only to raise a false alarm.

He didn't bother to rouse King to tell him, thinking the disappointment would only hurt him.

Around 2 p.m. he thought he saw something that looked rather strange. It was a black blob rising up out of the ice and he didn't know what it was. He looked again then said out loud, "that looks funny."

He stood upon the highest piece of the frame that they were sitting near and had a better look.

"It's smoke," he said.

Captain Kennedy heard him.

"What did you say?" he asked.

Sargent was surprised that the captain had heard him, he thought he was in a coma.

"I can see smoke in the distance, Captain."

The Day of Varick Frissell

"Are you sure it's smoke?" Kennedy asked in a pitiful tone of voice.

Sargent shaded his eyes then looked again.

"Yes, there is no doubt about it, sir. It's smoke."

"Then it's a ship," Kennedy said quietly. "But don't wake Clayton yet, the longer he's unconscious the less pain he will have to bear."

Sargent agreed, but the excitement was almost too much to keep contained.

"We should be rescued in about a couple of hours," said Kennedy.

"I hope so," said Sargent, then he almost went wild.

The Sagona was now going at full speed through the ice heading for the Viking disaster site.

One of the men on the upper bridge said, "I think I see something, Skipper"

"Where?" asked Skipper Jake.

"Out there," said the sailor, pointing.

"Something is on the port bow," called the lookout from up front.

"Where away?" asked Skipper Jake.

"Board on, sir!! Board on," said the man standing in the rigging.

"What is it?" the captain roared.

"A flag, sir, it looks like a flag," said another man.

"Jingles, men, where to?" demanded the skipper.

"There's a flag of some sort flying from a stick out there on an ice pan, I can see it," said the man on the lookout.

"Hand me them glasses, mate," said the skipper.

The mate handed him the glasses and he took a look.

"There are two men standing on a ice pan, sir," said the man on the lookout.

Jacob Kean looked closer with the glasses.

"No, I can see three men, one of them is lying down," he said. and excitement rose on the Sagona.

"Tell the doctors there are three men up ahead on a ice pan," said the captain.

Sargent could not control himself. He started yelling and jumping up and down.

Clayton King told his story this way. "I was awakened out of my unconscious state by screaming and yelling. It was Sargent yelling and screaming."

"Was the man going out of his mind or something?" Clayton whispered.

"There's a steamer! Yes, there's a steamer coming. I can see her hull, and she's coming right at us, Clayton."

Clayton thought Sargent had gone out of his mind, he knew that a man could only take so much before he cracked, but yet!

His tone of voice sounded different. It wasn't like a man insane, it sounded real.

"What's wrong, Sargent?" asked Clayton in a low tone of voice, but clear.

"There's a ship coming, we can see her in the distance."

"Lift me up so I can see her if you can, Harry."

Clayton said that from that very moment he began to feel stronger. As Sargent lifted him up he saw her. The huge billow of black thick smoke was reaching into the sky.

"Could this be possible?" said Clayton. "Yes, she was coming, thank God it was real. The ship was drawing near. Although I was dying yet I felt a thrill run through me as I recognized the good old ship Sagona."

Those on board watched from the deck of the Sagona as the ship drew nearer to the ice pan that looked like a pile of debris. And right in the center they saw smoke rising from a small fire that had been the savior of the men on the ice pan.

The men's flag was waving in the wind as they drew closer. The captain yelled to the men.

"We can't get too close to the pan because there's too much swell in the water, we could strike it and knock it over."

The ship was stopped about a hundred feet away.

"Launch a dory, Mate, and man it," Jacob yelled.

"Aye aye sir," said the mate.

Everyone was on deck now, even the cooks.

Three men got in the dory and the Sagona's crew hoisted the boat over the side. When the dory hit the ice, three more men climbed down over the side and in. It took only a few minutes for the six men to reach the three Viking survivors. Clayton King said as the dory drew near to the stern part of ship that had been blown off from the Viking one of them yelled.

"Boys. Just smell that dynamite."

But when they saw King's broken legs, one said, "Oh my God! Look at King's legs, the bones are sticking out." And with this, they lifted him up and put him in the dory and hoisted him up and onto the deck of the Sagona, into safety.

After the doctors and nurses took control of the patients, the captain sent a wireless telegram to the Minister of Fisheries.

Radio Dispatch,

To Mr. H. B. Clyde Lake.
Minister of Marine & Fisheries,
St. Johns, Newfoundland
March 18th, 1931.

Picked up three men adrift on ice-pan and part of ships stern, fifteen miles east south east of Cape John, Gull Island. Men are----- Clayton King, radio operator. Navigator Captain Kennedy. And an American named Sargent.

(Sgn) Master S. S. "Sagona"

Chapter Forty-three

Captain Peter Carter of the S.S. Beothic, was searching for survivors from the ill-fated Viking. His location was between Horse Islands and Grey Islands in heavy ice.

His ship had been searching all day without seeing any trace of anyone or anything. He had been listening to wireless signals from various ships, informing each other what they were doing as far as searching for the Viking survivors.

The Beothic was about to burn down for the evening when someone saw a light far up ahead in the direction of the Grey Islands.

"What do you think of that, Captain?" said one of the officers on the bridge.

The captain went outside to get a better look at what it was.

"Someone is out there for sure," he said.

"You're right" said the officer.

"Okay," he said, "alert all the crew and the look outs and let's head in the direction of the light. And tell the mate to come up on the bridge. I think he went for a mug-up."

"Aye aye sir," he said.

It only took a few minutes for the Beothic to alter its course and head in the direction of the light. After going toward the light for about a mile, the captain asked the mate to start blowing the horn.

"Whoever is there will hear us. This will keep their courage up for sure," the captain said.

They steamed through the ice for about an hour but got no closer to the light. It seemed to keep ahead of the ship at the same pace.

"That's funny," said the mate.

"Yes, that looks awful queer to me too," said Captain Carter. "It must be a weather light or something."

As they were talking, their wireless operator heard the Sagona send a message about how they had picked up three people belonging to the Viking, in the vicinity of Cape John.

Everyone was excited to hear this news. At least there was still people being rescued, but this light?

"What does this mean, Mate, should we still keep chasing it? I don't know what we should do, maybe we should stop the ship and see what happens," said the captain.

"The ice is pretty good here now for men to travel on. We should put out a group of men and let them have a look," said the mate.

"Sounds like a good idea," said the skipper.

Captain Carter was no fool. In fact, he was one of the high liners in the sealing industry. He was captain on the ship that brought in the most pelts of any vessel that ever went to the ice.

They stopped the Beothic and put out twenty men, with the mate, on the ice floes. They let the men walk on ahead following the light for about three miles. Then they started up the ship and went ahead and picked them up. It was now after dark. When the men came aboard they reported seeing nothing, only the light that kept ahead of them.

"I can't understand it, Skipper," said the mate.

"No more can I," Carter said, "It's the first time that I have heard talk of anyone seeing a weather light in the daytime."

Captain Carter then sent the following wireless.

Minister of Marine and Fisheries,
St. Johns, Newfoundland.
March 18th, 1931.
Our search party returned to the ship at 10.30 p.m.
With nothing to report. Seeing a light that went before them, but was unable to catch it, although they followed it for several miles. Will keep you informed.
      (Sgn) Carter.... Beothic.

Chapter Forty-four

Pat Breen fought his way from the top of the engine room of the Viking to the main deck. Wreckage was everywhere, blocking all doors. He heard the roaring of flames and many more explosions. As he crawled along the deck, he met members of the crew, they were disoriented, not knowing which way to go.

"Over this way," he shouted loudly. But the roar of the fire was so great he knew they couldn't hear him so he made signs telling them which way to go.

When they got to the side of the ship and further away from the heat of the flames, he saw dories stacked on the deck.

"Let's launch those dories, men," he yelled.

It was obvious to him that they just wanted to get off the ship alive. They were afraid of another explosion that could trap them.

"Come on, men, let's get those dories off before the fire gets to them," he said as he finally persuaded them to help. "We will launch the ones that have not been damaged."

Although his two hands had been burned, Breen knew he would have to use them. The men got two of the undamaged dories over the side and onto the ice where others were waiting. Breen jumped down and pulled them clear of the side of the ship.

When this was done he heard someone on board the ship screaming for help.

Breen immediately boarded the ship again and crawled along the burning deck to where a couple of men were trapped under heavy timber. He lifted the timber off using brute strength. Freeing the two men, he assisted them along the deck to the railing and pushed them over the side.

He jumped down and helped them away from the side of the burning ship. Breen took a look around. He saw Captain Kean lying on the ice in terrible pain. He went to him and asked him if he knew which direction land lay from where he was. Kean pointed in the direction of the land.

They picked up the captain and put him in one of the dories and pulled him safely away from the burning ship. As they were standing there they saw a man come out of the forward section and jump out onto the ice. It was Harry Brown, one of the night cooks.

"Harry, over here," said Kean. Harry recognized the voice.

"Yes, Captain, what is it?" he asked.

"You're going to have to go back on board and get some food for the men," said Kean.

"Okay, Captain," said Brown.

With that, Harry Brown went back on board the Viking. The men on the ice thought that they would never see him again.

Brown went into the burning galley and came back out with a armful of bread. He threw it over the side. He then rushed forward and assisted a man off the ship.

Brown went back again to the galley and this time he came out with some canned goods.

As he stood on the deck there was a large explosion and Brown was thrown off the ship onto the ice, where he received serious injury to his back and legs.

The Day of Varick Frissell

I suppose the acts of heroism that took place the night the Viking exploded will never be told because almost all the people that were involved are now long gone. In reading the bits and pieces that have been written about it it's difficult to get a window into what happened. For those that remain the events have been erased from their memories. Forever.

Chapter Forty-five

"Nicholena," said Varick.

She looked at him with tearful eyes then replied, "Yes Varick, go on with your story."

"After Sarah left me, I heard the noise of a ship, it had to be the Viking. I did not want to go near to her again. Cabot was pulling me through the water and I was floating right along. There were times when the light would come back and we would move smoothly along again. After we went for quite a while I heard voices calling out. But I did not answer. Then I heard a ship blowing its horn. Finally it got dark and Cabot came near me and I went to sleep. I don't know how long I slept but I was awakened by my mother calling out to me.

She said, "Varick, they say that you were killed out on the ocean and your body will never be found. I only pray to God that your body will be found some day and that you will get a Christian burial. With that, my mother started crying.

"I tried to speak to her but I couldn't. I was now out in eternity, drifting along with no one to put me at rest. I don't know how long I drifted in the ocean among the ice.

Cabot had full control of that. Finally I saw that I was near some shore. I remember the rocks very clearly. Cabot held me by the shoulder very tightly. He then pulled me ashore.

It seemed that my body was only a shadow. It looks as though only my bones were in the clothes.

Cabot pulled me up on land and straightened out my legs and arms. I watched him as he dug a hole in the ground and then pulled me over into it and with his hind legs covered me over."

Varick was wiping tears from his face as he stood there. Nicholena thought that he was going to fall. She went to him and put her arms around him and said,

"Just get hold of yourself and finish your story, Varick."

He wiped his eyes and looked in the vicinity of the Horse Islands, and said in a calmer voice,

"My dear, I have been here now for about seventy one years according to what you have told me. Although I have been here for a long time, yet I have been like the flowers. I come awake every spring and try to get in contact with someone who comes to this piece of ground every year. I remember I almost got the attention of a man in uniform one day. He was here with a woman working on these boxes when I called to him. He heard me but thought it was someone else calling him, and he left, I think it was the same man that was with you when you came just now.

Varick then walked over to one of the duck boxes and sat down. He looked around then smiled, "It feels so good to be alive again, Nicholena, even if it's only for a brief period. The air is so fresh and warm. The flowers smell so sweet. I think I can hear the sound of birds singing. It's a shame that our film crew got killed on the Viking, Nicholena."

Nicholena knew the story about the Viking. But could she tell him about what had happened?

She started crying.

He knew that she had something to tell him. He put his arm around her and said.

"My dear, you can tell me anything that you want too, in fact, I want to know, especially if it's something about the Viking."

Nicholena then told him as much about the Viking as she knew.

She said, "Your close friend, Harry Sargent, survived the explosion that day, and so did Clayton King."

She could have told him more about Clayton, how he lost his two legs, but lived to be an old man with crutches. But she couldn't.

She could have told him that Captain Kennedy died of pneumonia on the Sagona, the very ship that rescued him, before they got him to hospital. But she couldn't.

She could have told him about Penrod and Noseworthy, how they perished in the explosion and their bodies were never found. But she couldn't.

She could have told him that twenty-seven men got killed that dreadful night in the explosion on the Viking, and that Uncle Harry Brown spent the rest of his life a cripple, unable to make a living for his family. But she couldn't and wouldn't.

Varick Frissell would never know about this.

It was better for him to go on his journey not knowing what the end of the Viking really was.

But, in tears, she told him that when they came and told his mother about the explosion and that he was missing, she took sick. She told him that a few days after his mother received the news that he was dead and the search parties could not recover his body the news was so heart breaking to her that she went to bed and passed away that same night.

Varick put his head down into his hands and started crying. He stood up then and reached down and pulled her up to him and kissed her and held her tight.

"Nicholena, it's time for me to go, someone is coming. I hear a noise in the distance." He turned to her and said, "I have come back here to you for a reason. There has never been a memorial service held for me or the rest of the Viking crew near the Horse Islands, and for that reason we are wandering

The Day of Varick Frissell

out there in eternity with no rest. When the wildlife officer comes, ask him if he will bury me, please."

By now he was in tears, crying like a baby. Then he stopped and said, "I wonder what ever happened to Cabot."

While researching this story I went to Conche, Newfoundland, and talked to the great Paddy O'Neill. When I went to his house he was sitting on the couch smoking his pipe. After we had chatted, I told him I was writing about an American who came to the Northern Peninsula in the 1920's with Dr. Wilfred Grenfell.

I asked him if he ever heard of a man by the name of Varick... and he stopped me there, and said, "Frissell."

Well, to say the least, this grand old gentleman knew what I wanted to hear. I asked him if he ever heard anything about Frissell's dog, Cabot, coming ashore on the Grey Islands.

He replied, "Earl, I know all about that. This is about Frissell's dog." Paddy then told me the story.

The story has it that one day Uncle John Flynn of Grey Islands went out to Green Island in the early spring, probably the last week of May, to check his vegetable garden, that is, to see how much land he would be sowing this year, and see if any kelp had washed ashore in the storms.

He landed on the beach and walked ashore to his long beds that he had sowed the year before. When he had checked everything, he walked up to the hill that overlooked the harbor of Grey Islands. As he walked along he heard a dog barking.

"My," he said, "I wonder where a dog came from out here especially at this time of year."

Uncle John looked closer and there the dog was sitting down upon the moss not far from him. For a moment he got scared. Then he whistled to him and this large Newfoundland dog started wagging his tail. He walked closer and called out to him. He then went to him and patted him on the head.

He noticed that the dog was very skinny and also looked sick and couldn't walk without staggering. He could hardly stand.

"Someone owns you for sure," he said. He then noticed a leather collar around the dog's neck. Uncle John bent down and examined the collar. On it was a nameplate that read, "CABOT FRISSELL."

He noticed that the dog was in a very bad condition.

His back appeared to have been broken and healed. He also had a large scar on his side.

"I wonder what ever happened to you, Cabot?" he asked. Uncle John thought about the dog. He had eight dogs of his own that he used for hauling firewood. The people around had to be very careful about strange dogs in them days, especially one that was sick. It could have distemper, a disease that could wipe out all the dogs on Grey Islands.

Uncle John decided then what he would do.

"I am going to go back home and get some food and bring it out to you," he said.

Cabot wagged his tail as Uncle John left.

"You wait here, Cabot, till I come back."

Uncle John left and went in and got food for the large Newfoundland dog. But when he came back the dog was gone and they never saw him again.

Chapter Forty-six

Nicholena Leonardo stood near one of the eider duck boxes. She knew that this giant of a man, six foot eight inches tall, would soon have to leave. Her mind was in a swirl.

"No one would ever believe me," she thought.

Varick walked upon the little rise that was near the water and called to her to come and stand near him for a moment.

He reached down and picked a handful of bakeapple blossoms and held them in his hands, then said.

"I want you to place those on my grave after you have buried me, Nicholena. And every spring when those blossoms come out in bloom, I want you to remember me."

She promised him she would.

"Listen, my dear," he said, "I want you to stand near me for a minutes silence in honor of my friends who were killed so carelessly on the Viking. And may God rest their souls."

As they were standing silently together, they could hear the outboard motor coming in the distance.

The wildlife officer was on his way to get Nicholena and take her back to the cabin.

Varick walked to the shallow grave where Nicholena had dug him out as a skeleton. He stepped over near her and put his arms around her and kissed her.

The Day of Varick Frissell

She looked at his eyes and knew that there was something wrong. His eyes began to look old.

She felt his arms when they began to shiver and get weak. She noticed that he was beginning to bend over.

"My God," she cried, "is this for real?"

Then she felt a hot tear fall from his eyes and drop on her neck.

"Goodbye forever, Nicholena, my dear," he said in a quivering voice. "You will never see me again."

He gave a great sigh then said, "I want you to turn around and look to the westward again, my dear."

Nicholena turned and looked to the westward, but only for a moment. When she turned around Varick Frissell was no more. She looked, and he was only a skeleton in a shallow grave. She immediately took the shovel and started covering the skeleton. She felt as though she was hiding something. In just a few minutes it was all covered over. She placed the white blossoms on the grave and broke down and wept.

She heard the game warden coming. He was singing as he came over the hill.

"Nicholena. Nicholena," he called.

She called back, "I'm here, over here, Christian."

He hurriedly came to where she was, but before he got close to her he sensed that there was something wrong.

He stopped. Seeing the tears on her face he asked, "What's wrong, my dear? I knew I should have never left you here alone by yourself all day."

He was shocked to see her crying.

"Are you hurt or something?"

"No, not physically," she sobbed.

"Well, what's wrong?" he demanded.

"Sit down, please, there is a story I must tell you about what happened to me today, and afterwards you have to do something."

The wildlife officer sat down and Nicholena told him the whole story about what had happened that day.

After Nicholena had told him the story and what Varick Frissell's last request was, he stood with his head bowed and hands folded and looked at the disturbed ground nearby.

"I don't think you believe me, sir," she said with tears in her eyes.

"This is a troubled girl," he thought to himself. She must be running from something.

"I believe you, my dear, and I am going to read the burial the best way that I know how. I am not a minister, but I'll do my best"

"Thanks," she said, as she wiped away her tears.

"Just a moment," she said, as she picked up the CD player and took the earphone plug out of the small machine so the two of them could hear what was being played.

And as Don Williams started singing, "Lord I hope this day is good, I feel empty and misunderstood," the wildlife officer picked up a handful of mud and started the burial by quoting from the Book of Job 19:25,

"I know that my Redeemer liveth and that he will stand again upon the earth in the last day. This grave will never hold me, in that moment I'll be gone, and though the worms destroy this body of mine, yet in my flesh shall I see God."

Nicholena stood motionless, as the officer continued, "In the name of God and the Holy Trinity I commit the body of Varick Frissell to the ground."

He held the handful of mud over the grave and sprinkled it, he then said, "Ashes to ashes and dust to dust. May Varick Frissell and the rest of the Viking victims rest in peace and may God have mercy on their poor souls."

As soon as he said "Ashes to ashes and dust to dust." they heard a noise upon the hill. They both looked. Then they heard it clearly. A dog barked three times. It was Cabot.

Christian looked out toward the Horse Islands in the glow of the setting sun. It was 9 p.m. He turned to the young woman standing near him and said, "Truly, this was The Day of Varick Frissell."

Varick, as a toddler with his Father

Varick with his Mom and Dad

The Day of Varick Frissell

Varick Going Fishing

*The Frissell Children
Toni, Varick and Monty*

Varick in his teens

The Day of Varick Frissell

Varick in St. John's

The Day of Varick Frissell

SS Viking in ice

Sealers on the Ice

CREW AS APPEARING IN SHIP ARTICLES.

Captain Abram Kean Jr., Brookfield, Master; Alfred Kean, Brookfield, Second Hand; David Winter, Valleyfield, Master Watch. J. J. Wheeler, Lower Island Cove, 1st Master Watch; W. G. Johnstone, Job's Cove, Master Watch; George Day, Little Harbor, P. B., Bridgemaster; Henry Brown, 17 MullockStreet, Galleyman; William Goodwin, Trinity Bay, First Cook; Alfred Butt, Freshwater, Bridgemaster; Robert Cole, Conception Hr.; Michael Martin, Flatrock; Alphonsus Doyle, Gull Island; Israel Foley, Bonavista; Chesley Martin, Bonavista. James Street, Bonavista; Yetman Mouland, Bonavista, Wm. Bartlett of John, Georgetown, Brigus,Wm. Cole, Colliers; Walter Batten, Bareneed; Herbert Ryan, Port Rexton; Michael Martin, Torbay; Jacob Bradbury (Thom.), Torbay; Nicholas Roache, Middle Cove; Dan Fleming, Spillar's Cove; Isaac Bradbury, Brigus; Michael Kinsella, Outer Cove; Edward Spracklin, Brigus; James Coady, Outer Cove; George Cross, Badger's Quay, John Soper, Carbonear; Fred Percey, Brigus; Arthur Richards, Brigus; Abram Dyke, 22 Beaumont Street; Albon Oakley, Wesleyville; Walter Power, Flatrock; Stephen Lush, Georgetown, Brigus; James Linthorne, Georgetown, Brigus; John Whitty, Georgetown, Brigus; John Ryan, Logy Bay; Malcolm Webber, Cupids; Jerry Quinlan, Red Head Cove; Frank Dawe, Bay Roberts; George Linthorne, Georgetown, Brigus; Arch Linthorne, Georgetown, Brigus; John Breaker, Brigus; Roland LeGrow, Bauline; James Burke, Colliers; Benj. Ganey, Colliers; Ernest Newell, Burnt Head; Richard Conway, Colliers; Alfred Fifield , Trinity; Henry Sparkes, Georgetown, Brigus; Robert Bartlett, Marysvale; Harold Bishop, Burnt Head; James Dawe, Burnt Head; Richard Fowler, Burnt Head; William Fowler, Burnt Head; John Newell , Georgetown, Brigus; John Boland, Calvert; James White, Greenspond; Joseph Kelly, Brigus; James Fey, Brigus; Sydney Burry, Greenspond; John Gosse, Torbay; Patrick Brown, Colliers; Charles McGrath, Colliers; Joseph Cole, Colliers, Patrick Burke, Colliers; Joseph Brown, Colliers; Albert Sparkes, Sibley's Cove, T. B. ; Joseph Lambert, King's Bridge Road; Edward Conway, Colliers; Jacob Ralph, Brazil's Square;

Harold Batten, Bareneed; Wm. R. Boones, Bareneed; William Fleming, Bonavista; James Murray, Pouch Cove; Jacob Newell, Pouch Cove; Tom Fleming, Bonavista; Israel Pearce, Bonavista; David Chaulk, Catalina; Gordon Loveys, Western Bay; Stanley Johnston, Job's Cove; Eli Garland, Caplin Cove, C.B. ; Simeon Garland, Caplin Cove, C. B. ; Edward Oliver, Gull Island, C. B. James Oliver, Gull Island, C. B. ; Joseph Oliver, Gull Island, C. B. ; Michael Martin, Flatrock; Nanshi Tippett, Catalina; Isaac Efford, Bareneed, C. B. ; Vincent Hawco, Torbay, Henry Codner, Torbay; Peter Berg, Wesleyville; Joseph Stockley, Brookfield, B. B. ; Victor Hicks, Bonavista; Albert Spracklin, Brigus; George Efford, North River; Zack Thistle, Pouch Cove; Walter Bursey, Lower Island Cove, C. B. ; Frank Flynn, Brigus, Ira Pearcy, Brigus; Thomas Kennedy, Brigus; Simon S. Spracklin, Brigus; Noah Way, Bonavista, Alfred Way, Bonavista; Wilson Kennedy, Western Bay; Ernest Spracklin, Brigus; Edward Dalton, Western Bay; Paddy Spracklin, Brigus; Walter Crew, Flatrock; William John Doyle, Gull Island, C. B. Dan Brown, Brigus; John Roberts, Brigus; Fred Payne, Brigus, George Adams, Brigus, Edward Bragg, Pouch Cove; Ronald Gushue, Brigus; John Kennedy, Brigus; George H Youden, Brigus; Richard Walker, Brigus; John Doyle, Gull Island, C. B.; Ben Antle, Brigus; Patrick Bartlett, Brigus; Samuel Morgan, Seal Cove, Henry Sparkes, Brigus; George Spracklin, Brigus; Thomas Spracklin, Brigus; Charles Spracklin, Brigus; William Kennedy, Job Street, Navigator; John J Roche, Top Battery Road, Doctor; Clayton King, Brigus, Marconi Operator; A James Young, 26 McNeil Street, Food Inspector; Stephen Mullett, Westeyville, Store Keeper; Ronald Carter, Pleasant Street, Boatswain; Joseph Murphy, 29 Cabot Street, Chief Engineer; Fred Carnell, Quidi Vidi Road, Second Engineer; H. Hansford, Shaw''s Lane, Third Engineer; Firemen: P. Whalen, 18 Spencer Street; Patrick Breen, 45 Flower Hill; John Burke, 18 Spencer Street; Richard Adams, 19 Brennan Street; Harold Wiseman St. West, Anthony Taylor, MacFarlane Street. Movie men: Varick Frissell, A. E. Penrod, Harry Sargent, and helper (probably Noseworthy)

MISSING

Varick Frissell, New York
A. E. Penrod, New York
E. Cronin (stowaway) St. John's.
David Winter, master-watch, Valleyfield.
J. Wheeler, master-watch, Lower Island Cove.
William Goodwin, cook, New Melbourne.
Charles Fry, cook, Brigus.
George Cross, Badger's Quay.
Alban Oakley, Wesleyville
James Linthorne, Georgetown, Brigus
John Austin, Brownsdale
Malcolm Webber, Cupids (may be on Thetis)
John Breaker, Brigus
Joseph Kelly, Brigus
Joseph Stockley, Brookfield
Zach Thistle, Pouch Cove.
Patrick Bartlett, Brigus
Henry Sparkes, Brigus.
George Spracklin, Brigus.
Stephen Mullett, Wesleyville.
John J. Roche, St. John's.
Roland Carter, Pleasant Street, St. John's
Joseph Murphy, St. John's
Fred Carnell, St. John's.
H. Hansford, St. John's.
Harold Wiseman, St. John's
Anthony Taylor, St. John's

Over the years Earl Pilgrim, who is undeniably Newfoundland and Labrador's favourite storyteller, has been the recipient of many awards. In 2002 he received the Queen Elizabeth II Golden Jubilee Medal for his work as a game warden and for his writing.

He has received the Safari International award from the provincial Wildlife Division, the Gunther Behr award, which was presented by the Newfoundland and Labrador Wildlife Federation, and the achievement "Beyond The Call of Duty" award, presented by the White Bay Central Development Association.

Earl has also made a hobby of raising eider ducks and it has been estimated eighty percent of all nesting eider ducks in Newfoundland developed from his original dozen.

WHERE IS EARL B. PILGRIM NOW?

Earl and his son Norman have a wilderness lodge in the mountains of the Cloud River on the Great Northern Peninsula of Newfoundland and Labrador.

They do big game hunting for moose, caribou and black bear during the fall, and snowmobiling during winter.

They also do trout and salmon fishing during summer. It is to be noted that the area where they hunt and fish is one of the most successful on the island. And, the location where they snowmobile is the finest.

Earl can be reached by calling 709-457-2041
cell 709-457-7071 or email earl.pilgrim@nf.sympatico.ca
Norman can be contacted at 709-457-2451 or
cell 709-457- 7117, 709-457- 7038.
web address is www.boughwiffenoutfitters.com